Hummingbird Heart

Hummingbird Heart

ROBIN STEVENSON

ORCA BOOK PUBLISHERS

Library and Archives Canada Cataloguing in Publication

Stevenson, Robin, 1968-
Hummingbird heart / Robin Stevenson.

Issued also in electronic formats.
ISBN 978-1-55469-390-0

I. Title.
PS8637.T487H84 2012   JC813'.6   C2011-907422-2

First published in the United States, 2012
Library of Congress Control Number: 2011942576

Summary: Dylan is sixteen when she first meets her father,
who is looking for a donor match for his sick toddler.

*Orca Book Publishers is dedicated to preserving the environment and has printed
this book on paper certified by the Forest Stewardship Council®.*

Orca Book Publishers gratefully acknowledges the support for its publishing programs
provided by the following agencies: the Government of Canada through the Canada Book
Fund and the Canada Council for the Arts, and the Province of British Columbia
through the BC Arts Council and the Book Publishing Tax Credit.

Cover design by Teresa Bubela
Cover artwork by Janice Kun
Author photo by David Lowes

ORCA BOOK PUBLISHERS   ORCA BOOK PUBLISHERS
PO Box 5626, Stn. B   PO Box 468
Victoria, BC Canada   Custer, WA USA
v8R 6s4   98240-0468

www.orcabook.com
Printed and bound in Canada.

15 14 13 12 • 4 3 2 1

To Maggie Bird

one

I balanced the camera on a stack of books and squinted through the viewfinder, trying to line up the shot so that my mom and Karma were near the center and the teetering pile of books and papers on the end table wasn't visible.

"Hurry up." Karma shifted her position, crossing her ankle over her knee and leaning forward. "Just take a picture already."

"I'd be done already if you didn't keep talking." My finger hovered over the button. "Mom? Could you at least smile a little?"

"My face is starting to ache." She brushed her hair back over her shoulder. "Okay, fine." She bared her teeth. "Cheese."

I set the timer, ran to the couch and crouched between them. *Click.*

The smile slid from Mom's face. "Christ. Enough." She stood up and stretched. "You do know you're wasting your time, right?"

I shrugged and looked at the photo on the tiny screen. "Want to see it?"

Karma took a quick peek and made a face. "I look like Kermit. The lighting in here's weird. Greenish."

"Let me see." Mom took the camera from me and studied the picture, frowning slightly.

"You're the photographer, Mom. If you want to do it…"

"I didn't say anything. Anyway, I don't *do* portraits. You know that."

No kidding. If she did portraits, maybe we could afford to live somewhere halfway decent. As it was, Karma's room was barely big enough for her bed, the kitchen faucet dripped constantly, mold crept along the window frames and the downstairs neighbors grew marijuana in the shared backyard.

"Fine," I said. "I'll print it. You'll send it to him, right?"

She sighed. "He won't write back, you know. So don't get your hopes up."

"He might. You don't know."

"Well, he never has before." There was an unmistakable note of satisfaction in her voice.

I didn't say anything, because she was right. Every birthday since third grade I'd made Mom mail my father a photo of me. The first few times I used my school photo, but for the last three years I'd sent a family picture because sending one just of me felt sort of embarrassing. He'd never replied. I told Mom that I wanted to get to know him, but I wasn't sure if I meant it. Sometimes I wondered if I sent the pictures because I wanted him to feel guilty. Either way, I knew Mom didn't like it.

"Well," she said. She looked at me, her expression unreadable. "Sweet sixteen."

When she was sixteen, she was pregnant with me. It wasn't something she liked to talk about, but you didn't have to be a genius to guess that her memories weren't all happy ones.

Turning sixteen didn't change anything. I still had to go to school the next day. I frowned at myself in the dingy hallway mirror. Wrinkles. I leaned closer and stared at the two faint vertical lines between my eyebrows. They were barely visible, but they were most definitely there. It figured, what with the hole in the ozone layer, the pesticides in our food and the thousands of toxic chemicals coursing through our veins. I'd just read an article online about how my generation would be the first ever to have a shorter life span than the previous one.

"Pickle!" Mom yelled. "You're dragging your ass this morning. Do you need a ride?"

I frowned. In the mirror, my reflection frowned back at me and the lines deepened. "I'll take my bike."

My mother drove an ancient gas-guzzling, carbon-spewing station wagon. A few months ago, someone put a sticker on her car—while she left it idling somewhere, I figured, though she denied it—that read *I'm responsible for climate change.* She had laughed; then she'd sighed and said not everyone could afford hybrids and Smart cars. It took her awhile to get around to it, but she'd finally scraped the sticker off with nail polish remover and a dull kitchen knife.

In the kitchen, Karma was eating breakfast and Mom was sitting at the kitchen table, sketching. I grabbed a couple of slices of bread from the freezer and started making a peanut-butter sandwich.

Mom raised her eyebrows. "Tell me you're not eating that frozen."

"It'll thaw by lunchtime. What are you drawing?"

"Tattoo design."

I put down the frozen sandwich with a *thunk.* "You said you wouldn't get any more."

She opened her mouth to say something, but stopped and shook her head. "So? Maybe I changed my mind. Sometimes people do that, you know."

Karma looked at me and crossed her eyes.

I grabbed a sandwich bag and slammed the drawer closed, pinching the soft part of my little finger. I swore under my breath, shoved the sandwich in the bag and dropped it in my backpack. "I have to go."

"Pickle, don't be like that."

"I'm not being like anything. I don't want to be late, that's all." I avoided my mother's eyes. "And don't call me Pickle."

"Dylan…"

"I have to go," I repeated. I tossed my backpack over my shoulder and headed down the stairs and out the front door.

ᕋ

My mother was obsessed with tattoos. Some of her interests—like belly-dancing and tai chi—were short-lived, but the tattoos, of course, were permanent.

It wasn't like I had anything against tattoos. Plenty of kids at school had used their fake IDs to get them. Even my friend Toni's mother, who was close to fifty, had a small butterfly on her ankle. But my mother was up to nineteen. She had birds—bright red and green and blue birds—flying up the inside of both forearms. Her feet and ankles were a swirl of green and black vines. Her belly button was circled by a sun. A lizard stretched lazily across her shoulder and a tree spread its dark branches across her lower back.

And apparently she wasn't done yet.

I got on my bike, cycled hard toward school and tried not to care. Whatever. It was her body. If Mom wanted to look like a walking canvas, that was her choice.

Judging by the state of his own arms, her latest boyfriend wasn't going to have a problem with it.

❧

Toni waved from down the hall. "Dylan! How's it going?"

I hurried toward her so that she wouldn't try to have a conversation at full volume in front of half the school. "Hey."

She pushed her curly hair away from her face and tucked it behind her ears. It sprang back out the second she took her hands away. "How come you didn't call me last night?"

"Sorry. I…there was a lot going on." I lowered my voice. "Scott came over." One of the nice things about having the same best friend for a really long time was that you didn't always have to explain things.

"Really? Your mom's new…" Toni trailed off.

"Yeah. Her new whatever. We met downtown for dinner." I started walking slowly in the direction of class, and Toni looped her arm through mine in one of those casual gestures that seemed to come so easily to her. I was clumsy and awkward about that kind of thing; always elbowing someone, or standing too close, or not knowing how to let go again.

"So?" she asked. "What's he like?"

"Total freak."

"Details, please!"

I focussed on the obvious. "Tattoos from elbow to wrist, both arms. And lots of piercings." Other than the regular ones in ears and noses, I thought piercings were gross. Scott had piercings in his lips and tongue and eyebrow, and God only knew where else. Well, God and my mother, presumably, but I didn't want to dwell on that thought.

"What does he do? Does he at least have a job?" Toni knew my mom's track record. Her last boyfriend had "borrowed" two hundred bucks before taking off to Montreal.

"Yeah, that's how they met. He ran a group Karma was in at the Boys and Girls Club."

"Well, that's good, right? So he's—what? A counselor or something?"

"I guess. He's going to university. Social work." I shrugged. "But he used to be a drummer for some totally lame hardcore band, and he's still working the bad-boy image. It's pathetic."

"You should've texted me from the restaurant," Toni said. "Is he cute?"

"Come on, Toni. He's at least thirty." I didn't want to talk about Scott anymore, and kind of regretted having said anything. "Don't tell anyone, okay?"

"I won't. But I don't see what the big deal is."

"Of course not. You have a mother, a father, a minivan and a golden retriever. Your family is like an advertisement for normal."

"Uh, hello? Divorced, remember?"

"I know, I know." I grimaced apologetically. "I'm sorry. I shouldn't have said that."

"It's okay."

"It's just that I don't need one more thing to make me feel like I'm weird, you know?" I held up my hand and numbered off with my fingers. "One. My mother is totally—well, you know what she's like."

"She's cool," Toni protested. "Just kind of different. Quirky."

I snorted. Toni loved my mom, but she didn't have to live with her. "She smokes pot and takes photos of alleyways."

"Which win prizes in photography contests."

"Yeah, but they don't exactly sell. Anyway, let me finish." I held up a second finger. "Two. I have a sister who isn't really my sister. And her name is Karma. I mean, it's not like there aren't enough normal names out there to pick from. But no. Karma."

"Okay, okay." She gestured at me to get on with it.

"Okay. Um, three. I don't have a father. I have my mom's one-night stand. Sperm donor guy." That was what my mother had called him. *Just think of him as a sperm donor*, she'd said. *No regrets because otherwise I wouldn't have you, but don't you dare get pregnant at sixteen.* Since I'd never done more than kiss a guy—and barely even that— this hardly seemed likely. Mom said I was a late bloomer. I thought loser might be a more accurate description.

"Fathers aren't so great," Toni said.

I ignored her. "He's never even bothered to meet me." Toni didn't know about the photographs I'd sent him, but I knew what she'd say if she did. *Get a life, Dylan. He's not worth it.* "Mom says he was an asshole anyway."

Toni laughed but not unkindly. "And five, you have a best friend who thinks you're great."

"Which makes you almost as weird as me. Anyway, you can't count. That's four."

She ignored that and tilted her head to one side, considering. "You never know though. Amanda's new boyfriend could turn out to be an okay guy."

"Whatever." I shrugged. "He won't be around long anyway. You know my mom."

"Maybe this time will be different."

I doubted it. But then, Toni and my mom always said that I was a pessimist. I thought that both of them— like most people, really—were in denial most of the time. Look at the environment, for example. Everyone just carried on as if the entire human race wasn't on the edge of global disaster. It was insane. Sometimes, when I was trying to go to sleep at night, I'd picture the planet suspended in space, billions of people clinging to it like ants, the water being slowly poisoned, the ozone layer disintegrating, the ice caps melting, the oceans heating up, suicidal terrorists blowing planes out of the sky.

Think positive, Mom was always saying. *Look on the bright side.* But it seemed to me that there were all these possible futures and most of them looked pretty bleak. It was hard to feel hopeful in a world that was being destroyed.

TWO

I looked at the clock. Only five minutes into civics and the teacher had already succeeded in putting half the class to sleep. I rested my chin on my hands and watched the second hand ticking off the time.

Tick, tick, tick.

Sometimes I'd be doing this, waiting for time to pass, and I'd get a sudden clutch of anxiety. Every second that passed was gone forever. Every minute, every hour, every day. It was awful, imagining all that time slipping away, all those seconds rushing past in an unstoppable roaring stream. I could almost hear it when I closed my eyes. *Racing toward the grave.* I mean, of course everyone knew we were all going to die eventually, but no one else ever seemed to think about it.

I could remember precisely the first time I realized how temporary everything was. I was maybe eight or so, standing at the fall fair watching the lights of the Ferris wheel against the night sky, and it suddenly hit me that one day all of this would end. That I'd be dead and my mother would be dead and everyone here would be dead. All these people who were laughing with their friends, screaming around the curves of the roller coaster, eating snow cones...every last one of us would be burned to ashes or rotting underground.

I didn't know how to live with that. It seemed like you had to forget you knew it just to keep on going. But I couldn't seem to forget it the way everyone else did. After that first time, the same realization kept flashing into my mind. I'd be sitting in class, surrounded by people, and I'd think, Eventually, we'll all be dead. Or a bus would go by and I'd think, If I just stepped two feet to the left, that'd be it. Dead.

I didn't talk about it. In fact, I did my best to push the thoughts away. I didn't even like seeing the word *death*. If I came across it while I was reading, I'd flip pages like mad, trying to find a good word—*life* or *alive* or *living*— to cancel it out. And if anyone even mentioned death or cancer or car accidents, I'd start to feel all panicky and I'd have to make them change the subject somehow.

Someone kicked the back of my chair, and I turned around. Krista slid a piece of paper across her desk, hidden under her palm. I grabbed it and stuck it inside my binder. Mr. Robertson droned on about representative democracy, completely oblivious.

The note was from Toni and covered with smiley faces. I frowned. When had Toni started putting smiley faces on everything? She never used to do that. Back in junior high, we used to make fun of girls who did that. *Cheer up, it's Friday*, the note said. *Guess what? There's a party tomorrow night at Jessica's place. Guess who's going to be there? Hah. I'll tell you at lunch.*

I turned and raised my eyebrows at Toni, but she dropped her gaze to her textbook with a smug smile. I turned back to my own notes, but of course now I couldn't concentrate. There were two things that note could mean. One, Jax was going. Or two, something else entirely.

Jax was sitting at the end of my row, three desks away. The new kid. He'd just started at our school, and because he was gorgeous and also because arriving halfway through the first term was kind of unusual, everyone was curious about him. Toni was the only person who knew that I had a bit of a crush on him. Not that I'd admitted it, even to her, but she'd figured it out somehow. I slid my eyes sideways to steal a glimpse.

Blond hair but not too fair—kind of streaky brown and blond together, always hanging over his face until he shook it back out of his eyes. Tanned skin, perfect white teeth, a grin that narrowed his eyes and creased his cheeks with deep lines that were almost but not quite dimples. A careless attitude, which threw me off balance somehow. How could someone be new, not know a single person and walk around with that kind of confidence? I'd gone to school with these kids since kindergarten and still I felt like I didn't really fit in. I worried all the time about what other people thought of me.

I wrote Jax's name on the back side of Toni's note, over and over, in perfect letters so tiny that you'd need a magnifying glass to read them. I wrote it the way I always saw it: the *j* and the *x* small, the *A* capitalized and oversized, a tall point between them. A precisely balanced pyramid.

Then I crumpled the paper into a ball.

Jax would probably go for a girl like Toni: someone outgoing and fun. Someone who wasn't getting frown lines already. Someone who drew smiley faces on her notes.

❧

Lunch hour. I sat on the school steps, breathing in the crisp fall air. Across the street, a woman sat in the driver's seat of a parked minivan, engine idling while she waited, toxic emissions spewing from the car.

I hugged my knees to my chest. The sky was a clear blue with a few white puffs of cloud. It was strange, the way an ordinary day could suddenly seem so beautiful and so fragile it made you ache. Lots of things were like that though. Odd things, like a pair of white skates in the sports-store window, or a lone wildflower at the side of the road, or a glimpse of a Ferris wheel at night. Things that were so perfect they made you catch your breath. When I was younger, I'd tried to explain it to my mom and to Toni, but neither of them understood what I meant at all. I learned to keep my weird thoughts to myself.

Toni sauntered over, thick brown curls bouncing, a wide grin on her round face.

I shook off my thoughts. "Do you enjoy torturing me?"

She giggled. "Did you guess?"

"No."

"Jax." Toni's cheeks dimpled.

I'd probably be too shy to talk to him anyway. "How did you hear that?"

She drumrolled her hands against her thighs and paused dramatically. "He told me."

"You guys were talking?"

"I just saw him in the hallway with a bunch of guys from one of my classes and we all got talking."

It figured. Guys always talked to Toni.

"What? What's wrong?"

"Nothing. So, is Finn going too?"

"Course."

I studied Toni's face. I liked Finn. It would be hard not to: he was smart, interesting and a genuinely nice guy. Finn wasn't the problem. The problem was that since Toni had gotten together with him, she hadn't had a lot of time for me. I forced another smile. "Great," I said.

THree

When I got home from school, Karma was sitting on the front porch steps, taking apart her bicycle. Technically, we shared the porch with the couple who lived in the main floor—our apartment was the upstairs half of an old house that been converted to a duplex—but they were hardly ever around. Just as well, I thought, looking at the chain and gears and tools that littered the stone walkway.

"Again?" I hopped off my own bike.

Karma adjusted her baseball cap, leaving a streak of grease across her forehead in the process. "The gears keep slipping."

I wouldn't have had a clue how to fix my bike's gears when I was eleven. I still didn't have a clue. I looked past her to the open front door. "Is Mom home?"

"Nope. She went out with Scott."

"Oh."

Karma's voice was quiet. "You don't like it, do you?"

"What?"

"Amanda and Scott."

She always called Mom by her name and that was fine with me. In a weird way, it made me feel less like I had to share my mother, though of course I still did. Mom didn't mind either. In fact, she'd suggested that I call her Amanda too, but I'd refused. No one I knew called their parents by their first names.

I shrugged. "I don't care."

"You do too."

I hated it when she acted like she knew me better than I knew myself. "Shut up, Karma." I pushed past her and walked into the house.

"Check out her new tattoo design," Karma yelled after me. "She left her sketchbook in the kitchen."

I dumped my bag in the front hall, kicked off my shoes and then picked them up again and lined them up neatly side by side. It was different for Karma. Amanda wasn't really her mom.

❧

In the kitchen, I poured myself a glass of water and eyed the closed sketchbook on the table. Obviously, it was none of my business. My mother was big on respecting privacy. On the other hand, it wasn't like a tattoo design was exactly private. And Karma had already seen it. I ran my finger across the cover of the sketchbook, trying to decide. If I didn't look, I'd wonder about it all evening, and if I did, I'd feel guilty. I looked out the window and started counting. If a car drove by before I got to fifty, I'd look. If not, I'd just go up to my room.

One, two, three…It bothered me that Karma thought I had a problem with Scott. I wasn't narrow-minded or anything. Seven, eight, nine…I wasn't. I hated it when people made judgments based on appearances. Twelve, thirteen…A blue suv zipped past. I walked over to the sketchbook, flipped it open and turned pages to find the most recent sketches.

There it was. A skeleton playing drums. My breath hissed out from between my teeth.

"I figured you'd look," Karma said from the kitchen doorway.

"Karma, you are such a pain in the ass."

"Nice, isn't it?"

"No. It's stupid."

"I knew you had a problem with Amanda going out with Scott." Karma's chin was set, lower lip sticking out, eyes narrowed.

Karma had made it quite clear that she adored Scott. She'd met him first, and when he and Amanda hooked up less than a month later, she seemed to think she had engineered the whole romance herself.

"I don't have a problem with that, okay?" I looked at the drumming skeleton again. I had to admit, my mother could draw. "I just have a problem with her getting a tattoo that is going to announce it to the whole world," I said. "Especially since she and Scott will probably break up in a few weeks anyway."

"No, they won't."

"Yeah, they will." I knew exactly how it would all play out. They'd start arguing, Mom would say she needed some space, et cetera, and they'd take a break from seeing each other, which would turn out to be permanent. Mom would hang out with Julia, hit the bars, drink more than usual for a month or so, and then she'd meet someone else and start the whole process all over again. Only this time around Karma's heart would be broken, which made me furious. Mom should know better.

"I'd give it two weeks, max." I jabbed my finger at the sketch. "This is as stupid as getting a tattoo of someone's name."

"My mom did that," Karma said softly. "She had my name tattooed on her arm."

"I meant a boyfriend's name or whatever." I thought about the tattoo of a hummingbird that Mom got when she was pregnant with me. "Getting your kid's name is different," I said. "That's a permanent relationship, not just a temporary one. You're supposed to love your kid forever." I looked at Karma's dirty face and wished I could snatch the words back. "I'm sorry. I didn't mean…"

"It's okay," she said. "I know what you meant."

I looked down at the sketch again. At the bottom of the page, Mom had written in small block letters: *MW, OCEAN FRONT INN, 214.* I raised my eyebrows. Pretty ritzy. Mom's friends were more the Motel 8 type. "Who's staying at the Ocean Front?" I asked, wanting to change the subject.

Karma glanced at the paper and shrugged. "MW? No clue."

A car pulled into the driveway. Mom. "She's home," I said, snapping the sketchbook shut.

Karma craned her neck to see. "With Scott?"

"Alone."

"Are you going to ask her about the tattoo?"

"No." I eyed Karma's face and wondered what she was thinking. It was always so hard to tell. "Are you?"

Karma shook her head. "Don't tell her we looked."

⌒

Mom shrugged off her denim jacket and dumped a pile of photos on the kitchen table. "I'm making some of these into greeting cards," she announced. "Julia's started working at that gallery near your school. She's going to try to sell some for me."

Julia was an old friend of Mom's. She used to work in a vintage clothing store downtown, and she'd tried selling Mom's art from there too. The problem was that there just wasn't a huge market for Mom's photographs. Mom scorned anything that she considered "commercial," which seemed to mean anything that might actually earn money. Greeting cards were a step in the right direction, in my opinion.

"That's great," I said, a shade too enthusiastically. I scanned the pictures on the floor. Fire escapes and telephone wires. I wondered how many people really wanted greeting cards like that. What kind of occasion would you want them for? *Congratulations on getting your new phone connected? Condolences on your recent house fire?*

Mom looked up, caught my eye and quickly looked away. "Well, we'll see. I hired someone new today, anyway."

Mom had a cleaning business called Urban Organics. The *Organics* part was my idea—I thought she should be using all-natural cleaners, so when she and Julia started the business a few years ago, I helped her make all her own products. It wasn't really much of a business, just Mom and Julia and a few other women, mostly mothers of kids I'd gone to elementary school with. Mom did all the scheduling, and she still cleaned houses most days as well. She'd kept the old name, but these days, her cleaning products came from Costco, and there was nothing organic about them.

"Yeah? What's she like?" I asked. Mom tended to hire people either because she liked their politics or because she felt sorry for them.

"Nice. Friend of Julia's. Her ex had a drug problem and she's on her own, trying to support the kids. Anyway, she hasn't done cleaning before, but she needed the work, you know?" Mom grinned at me. "I think I'll pair her up with Katie. She can show her the ropes."

"I have to go," Karma said. "I have a baseball game. And I'm sleeping over at Ashley's, okay?"

"I remember. Have fun." Mom turned to me. "Just you and me tonight, chickie."

Usually, I was happy to get time alone with Mom. Karma had been living with us for three years, since her own mother died, and while we got along okay, I liked it when I had Mom to myself. But tonight, I wasn't so sure. There was something about the way Mom was looking at me—something about the forced cheeriness of her tone— that made me nervous.

Four

There was something so *cosy* about having routines, I thought, as I slid the creamy block of mozzarella across the sharp scalloped edges of the cheese grater. Beside me, Mom was slicing a heap of mushrooms. *Pizza night.* Before Karma came to live with us, Friday night was always pizza night. Unfortunately, Karma wasn't a fan of anything involving melted cheese. She said it was gross and stringy and complained that the smell made her gag. So that was the end of our weekly pizza night. Now, whenever it was just me and Mom, we always made pizza together. I loved it.

"Goddamn it." Mom dropped the knife and looked at her thumb for a second. "Knife slipped." She stuck her thumb into her mouth and used her free hand to refill her wineglass.

I made a sympathetic face and turned my attention back to the mozzarella. Something was definitely going on. Toni always said how cool it was, the way my mother was so young and talked to me like we were friends, but I didn't always think so. Mom had a tendency to give me way too much information, especially when it came to her boyfriends.

There were things you didn't want to know about your mother. Things you didn't want to talk about.

I knew it was wrong of me, but I couldn't help wishing she was more like other people's moms. She was thirty-three but looked younger, and people always thought she was my babysitter or my older sister. And I knew it was snobby, but I wished she had a more professional kind of job, like being a nurse or a teacher or something. I had no shortage of wishes: I wished she'd finished high school; I wished she'd stay single for a while; I wished she wasn't going to get another tattoo; I wished she didn't drink so much; I wished she didn't smoke pot.

Sometimes I felt like she was the teenager and I was the parent. Mothers, I thought, should be more reliable. More predictable. More *grown-up*.

"Mom? Do we have pineapple?"

No answer. I glanced sideways at her. "Yo, Mom? Pineapple?"

She was done with the mushrooms and was just standing there with the tomato-sauce spoon motionless in her hand.

"Earth to Mom? You're dripping sauce everywhere."

"What?"

I shook my head. "I asked you if we had any pineapple."

"I don't have a clue. Look in the cupboard."

"Fine. Don't bite my head off."

"It's been a long day."

"Whatever." I turned my back and rummaged in the cupboard. Cat food for a cat we don't have, canned mystery-meat ravioli, soup, beans. No pineapple. I snuck a glance at Mom. She'd knocked back that second glass of wine in less than a minute and was scratching the back of her hand, leaving a red welt. Something was definitely up. "All right," I said. "What is it? What's wrong?"

Mom stopped scratching and folded her arms defensively. "What do you mean?"

"Please." I fought the urge to roll my eyes.

"Look, I...I'm sorry. You're right; I'm distracted." She fingered the stem of her empty wineglass. "There's something I have to talk to you about."

"Is it about Scott?"

"No."

There was a long pause, and I felt an unexpected rush of fear: ice in the belly and an electric tingle shooting down my arms. What if it was something really bad? What if she had cancer? I stared down at the tablecloth still folded on the table and studied the embroidered flowers.

"Dylan?" Mom reached out and touched my arm. "Pickle…I had a rather weird phone call this morning."

I wondered if it was a teacher or something, but I hadn't done anything wrong that I knew of. Teachers generally liked me. "Who from?"

She hesitated. "Mark. From back east. Your…you know. He's in town. He wants to come and see us. To meet you."

A split second's relief—there was nothing wrong with Mom—and then the words sunk in. My *father*, even though Mom wouldn't say it, wouldn't ever call him that. My heart was doing something crazy, crashing around in my chest like it was trying to bust out. I could hardly breathe. Was it possible to have a heart attack if you were only sixteen?

"Dylan, you don't have to see him. I'll just call him back and tell him to get lost. You can say no."

I swallowed hard. "Why? Why does he want to see me?"

"I don't know."

"So he just suddenly got curious or something? Like, maybe he was bored one day and remembered, 'Oh yeah, I have this daughter. I wonder what she's like'?"

"I don't know." She hesitated; then she cleared her throat as if she was going to say something.

"What?"

She dropped her eyes, shook her head. "I really don't know."

"He just called? For no reason? Why?"

"Oh, Dylan. I've told you everything I know."

I just looked at her. Maybe she didn't know why Mark was here, but there was something she wasn't telling me. I'd put money on it.

"I have," she protested. "You know I haven't seen him since before you were born."

"I know. But...this is really weird."

"Tell me about it."

She'd never told me much about my father. *Just a one-night stand*, she'd said. *No one important.* She'd happily share all kinds of details about her current boyfriends— and I mean *way* too much information—but whenever I asked her anything about the guy who got her pregnant, she basically brushed me off.

Was he tall, like me?

Yes.

What color were his eyes?

Shrug. *It's too long ago, Dylan.*

Mom...

Blue. Okay? They were blue.

It was like pulling teeth.

I only had this one bad photo of him: Mom in denim cutoffs, looking very pretty despite being too skinny and having dyed black hair and heavy black eyeliner. Standing behind her, out of focus, was Mark.

All I could really tell about him was that he had brown hair and a blue T-shirt.

She wouldn't even tell me his last name, because she just didn't want me going online and searching for him. According to her, he was an asshole and a selfish prick who had never even wanted to meet me. End of story.

Only now he was here, in town. And he wanted to see me. I looked at my mother and blinked back my tears. "I guess you don't want me to meet him."

She shook her head. "It's up to you."

"I might not bother. You know, since he's never bothered before."

"That's fine then. Fine." That was all Mom said, but the expression that flickered across her face looked a lot like relief.

FIVE

Mom and I seemed to have some unspoken agreement not to talk about it again, which was fine by me. I didn't even want to think about it, though of course I did. It was hard to think about anything else. The air in the house seemed to be getting heavier and harder to breathe, full of the thick sour smell of unsaid things. By the time Saturday evening rolled around, I was desperate to get out of the house, even though parties weren't my favorite thing.

Toni was sitting on my bed, applying purple nail polish she'd borrowed from my mom. "What are you wearing?" she asked.

I looked down at my jeans and blue sweater. "This?"

Toni looked up from her fingernails and studied my face for a moment. "Okay, what's the matter?"

"Nothing." She might have money for a dozen different outfits but I did not. "You don't think this looks okay?"

"It looks fine." Toni gave me a scrutinizing kind of look. "It's just that usually we try on different things and…oh, you know." She blew out a breath of frustration. "Come on, Dylan. You're so not into this party. Just tell me what's wrong."

I opened my window. The nail polish fumes were stinking up my room. I tried to breathe shallowly and wondered why I hadn't phoned Toni last night after Mom told me about Mark's call. Usually I told her everything. "Just some stuff with my mom. You know."

Toni watched me, a mixture of hurt and irritation flickering across her face. She flapped her hands to dry the polish and said nothing for a long moment. Finally she shrugged. "Well, if you want to talk about it…"

"Thanks. But I'm fine." I sat down on the edge of the bed. "Okay. Maybe I should wear something else. What do you think?"

"Actually, you look gorgeous, as usual. And that shade of blue suits you." She tilted her head to one side thoughtfully. "You just need something…here, try this lipstick."

I took it and ran the color along my lips. I wouldn't share lipstick with anyone else—I was too germophobic— but Toni didn't count. "There. Better?"

"Perfect." She sighed, lower lip sticking out, blowing air upward so that her curly hair lifted off her forehead. "You are so beautiful, Dylan. Seriously. Sometimes I wonder why I hang out with you. I'm so totally jealous."

I didn't think I was beautiful at all. I was tall and kind of clumsy, with long straight brown hair and blue-green eyes. My mouth was too wide, my eyebrows too heavy; and I wasn't sure what I thought about the slight cleft in my chin. I did like my nose though, and at least my teeth were all right. I stared at my reflection and wondered for about the millionth time whether I looked anything like Mark. The lipstick was startling: dark red against my too-pale skin. I brushed my hair and held it away from my face for a moment, trying to see myself objectively; then I let it fall forward so that it partly covered one eye.

Maybe I would refuse to meet him. Let him see how it felt to be rejected.

⟋

The party was only a few blocks from my place, so Toni and I walked over together. Karma followed us for the first block. She was pretending that she was going for a bike ride, but she was just tagging along to be annoying. She was so good at it, you'd never guess she hadn't been a younger sister her whole life.

"Is your boyfriend going to be there?" she asked Toni.

"How exactly is that any of your business? Anyway, it's too dark for you to go for a bike ride. You don't even have a light on your bike." Toni made a face at her. "Shouldn't you be in bed, little girl?"

Karma was unfazed. "I'm fixing my light. Anyway, it's not even eight thirty yet. I bet Dylan's going to kiss boys. Are you, Dylan?"

"Karma! Get lost."

"I know what high school parties are like," Karma said, her bike wobbling on the sidewalk and almost hitting me. "My friend's sister goes to them all the time. Everyone gets drunk and makes out."

"Yeah? Well, I don't, okay? I'm not like that." I gave her handlebars a gentle shove.

Karma put her feet down as her bike started to tip over. "Don't do anything I wouldn't do."

I rolled my eyes. "Good*bye*, Karma."

She stood there for a minute before she hopped on her bike and sped off toward home.

"Sometimes I'm glad I'm an only child," Toni said.

"She just wants to be older already, you know?" A cool wind was blowing straight down the street, and I wrapped my arms around myself, shivering. Personally, I didn't think being sixteen was that great. It was true, what I'd told Karma: I wasn't the type to get drunk and fool around.

In fact, though I'd never admit this to her, I'd never fooled around with anyone. Parties made want to crawl out of my skin, run away and hide in a hole somewhere.

Still, this one should be okay. Jessica wasn't exactly a close friend, but I'd known her forever. We'd gone to elementary school together, ridden bikes around the neighborhood, trick-or-treated at each other's houses at Halloween. And besides, even though I didn't enjoy parties, I couldn't stand to miss them either.

"You have FOMO," Toni had told me when I tried to explain this. "Fear of Missing Out."

I'd nodded. That was it exactly. "It's lame. I mean, what exactly do I think might happen?"

"Oh, I don't know. Someone interesting might show up." Toni had raised and lowered her eyebrows. "Someone whose name starts with *J*, perhaps."

Jax. To me, names nearly always had a shape or a texture. I used to think everyone noticed this, but Mom and Toni both looked at me like I was nuts when I tried to explain, years ago, that Toni's name was square and solid, and Mom's name, Amanda, was round and as powdery soft as icing sugar. So maybe it was just me. Anyway, Jax was a pyramid-shaped name. Triangular and sharp-edged. The opposite of Dylan, which was sort of floppy and undefined.

"I wonder if Jax has a girlfriend," I said.

"Not as far as I've heard."

"Mmm. Well, it's not like he'd be interested. I'm probably not his type." I hoped Toni would argue with me.

She laughed, but there was something impatient about it. I knew she didn't like it when I sounded too insecure. Maybe she agreed that I wasn't the kind of girl a guy like Jax would date. Maybe she even wondered what she was doing hanging out with me herself. I wished I could take back my last words.

"Maybe not," she said. "But you never know."

"You think I'm not then? Not that it matters, but what do you think is his type? I mean, why do you think he wouldn't be interested?"

She just shrugged. "I don't even know the guy, Dylan. But if you like him, go for it. Anyway, lighten up, okay? The party should be fun."

I didn't know what was wrong with me. I just felt…flat. Blah. Not even remotely in the mood for a party. Not like Toni, who was fizzing with energy and anticipation. She was champagne and I was…I don't know. Diluted Kool-Aid, maybe. Or skim milk. Something boring and unappealing.

When we were younger, Toni and I hadn't really needed a lot of other friends. We'd played outdoors all summer, practicing on the monkey bars at the park for hours and riding our bikes to each other's houses. In the winter, we'd holed up in Toni's parents' rec room, back before the divorce, and played Dogopoly and Cranium, and designed weird futuristic worlds. Glass domes, underground tunnels, teleportation devices and just-add-water meals. We talked about how scientists would develop replacement body parts, how people would never have to die unless they chose to, how we would live together near the ocean and rescue stray dogs. Toni used to be crazy about dogs. Maybe it was dumb of me, but I'd thought things would go on that way forever.

Looking back, it seemed like the change had happened almost overnight, the summer before grade eight. Toni's parents had separated, and Toni suddenly began to transform herself into someone else. She shed the scruffy jeans and started wearing makeup and developed a certain giggling laugh that she only used around boys. Toni and I had always made fun of teenage girls and had sworn we'd never be like that ourselves. I'd seen it closing in around us, in the music and the TV commercials and the girls smoothing on lip gloss in the hallways before class, but I'd really believed we could escape it. I'd believed it right up until Toni changed.

It wasn't like I still wanted to play on the monkey bars. I'd have been happy hanging out at home or at the mall with Toni. But she'd had one boyfriend after another since eighth grade. I had tagged along—still Toni's best friend, but no longer the only one.

Toni dragged me along to parties, made me one of the group. If it wasn't for her, I'd probably be a social outcast. She did all the work and I coasted along behind, like a cyclist drafting a truck, sucked along in the slipstream. I should have been grateful, and most of the time I was.

But I still wished things could go back to how they used to be when we were twelve.

SIX

The party house was thrumming with music and swarming with people. Half the high school must have been there. Jessica waved to us from across the living room and made her way over. Her face looked oddly unfamiliar behind pale foundation and darkly made-up eyes. She'd been a total tomboy when we were kids, into baseball and dirt bikes, but now she seemed to be turning into this model-wannabe who wore tight clothes and thigh-high boots with stiletto heels. I felt as though I didn't know her anymore.

"Hey, guys." Jessica winked at me.

I nodded back. "Hi." I gestured at the crowds. "Lot of people." *Duh.*

"Yeah, yeah. Hey, you haven't seen Ian, have you?"

"We just got here," Toni said.

"He doesn't like parties," Jessica said, rolling her eyes. "He's probably hiding somewhere. I better go find him."

I knew how he felt. Toni elbowed me, and I could hear bottles clinking together in the bag slung over her shoulder. "There's Finn," she said.

I followed her gaze. Finn was walking toward us. I'd never been attracted to him, but I could see why Toni was. Dark curly hair, dark eyes, nice body. And a slight British accent. He'd moved to Canada when he was barely old enough to speak, which made me wonder if he might be at least partly faking it. I realized I was frowning and quickly adjusted my expression to something more neutral. "Well, I guess I better give you guys some privacy."

"You don't have to. Hang out with us. Seriously, Dylan, you don't have to always…"

I gave Toni a one-armed sideways hug and forced myself to smile. "I know when three's a crowd." I nodded at Finn as he joined us. "Hey, Finn. I've gotta go talk to someone. I'll catch you later, Toni."

Finn grinned at me. Toni shrugged, pulled a six-pack of coolers out of her bag and handed one to me. I took it and wandered off, feeling lost as I made my way out of the kitchen and through the crowded living room. I shouldn't have come. I really didn't like parties. I usually spent the whole time feeling awkward and uncomfortable, or sitting in a corner somewhere having an intense conversation with one other person, which was fine, but in that case why be at a party at all?

I found an empty window seat and sat down, watching the party like I was in the audience at a play. Front row, and hoping none of the actors would actually try to interact with me. I tipped a mouthful of Toni's cooler down my throat. Ugh. And about the color—what did they put in there to make it that toxic blue? It was probably carcinogenic. What would make anyone think it was a good idea for a drink to be that color anyway? I tucked my feet beneath me and stared at my shoes. I should just go home.

⟲

An hour later, I was still thinking the same thing, but for some reason I hadn't actually left. Instead, I'd had a boring conversation about computer games with a guy I didn't know and an even more boring conversation about school with a girl from my French class. I'd drunk another of Toni's coolers and watched from a distance as Toni and Finn made out on the couch. I was pulling my phone out of my purse, trying to decide how uncool it would be to text Toni that I was leaving, when I glanced up and saw Jax.

He really was gorgeous. Every time I looked at him, I felt as if my heart actually, literally, skipped a beat.

I watched him walk across the living room and look around a little uncertainly. I hesitated. I should wave. That would be what Toni would do. Instead, I looked away.

Which was totally the wrong thing to do, because he'd already caught me looking. Out of the corner of my eye, I could see him walking toward me. Would he think it was weird that I'd seen him and just looked away? I forced myself to turn toward him and smile. My cheeks felt hot.

"Finally, a face I recognize," he said. "Jessica invited me, but I haven't seen her anywhere."

"She's around," I told him. "Did you just get here?"

"Yeah. I had to work tonight. I just got off."

"Where d'you work?"

He grimaced. "Don't ask."

"That bad?"

"Mmm." He grinned. "Golden arches, weird red-haired clown guy, skinny gray burgers, scary secret sauce."

"Did you know that North Americans spend more on fast food than education?"

He laughed. "Doesn't surprise me."

"And all that meat too. It's terrible." *Nice one, Dylan. Insult the guy, why don't you?* "I don't mean that people who eat meat are terrible," I said quickly. "It's just that the industry isn't sustainable. I mean, it takes almost five pounds of grain to produce one pound of beef. That's just crazy."

Jax laughed again. "You're cute when you get all excited. I'm Jax, by the way."

"I know." I wasn't sure I liked being called cute. It sounded like a compliment but…There was a brief silence and I realized that I'd missed a cue. I hoped he wouldn't notice that I was blushing. "Oh. I'm Dylan."

He nodded and repeated my name as if he was making an effort to remember it. "Right. *Dylan.* Come on, let's get a drink."

I followed him through the living room and back into the kitchen, vowing to shut up. I looked around for Toni but couldn't see her anywhere.

Jax grabbed a couple of beers and handed one to me. "So," he said, turning back to me. "Let's go find somewhere to sit down."

My heart sped up. Was he coming on to me? Toni always said I was uptight. I knew I was. I couldn't help it. Look at me now—we'd barely had a conversation and already I was worrying about things. Sex things. Expectations. My cheeks burned. He probably wasn't even interested in me anyway. Not that way.

Jax chugged some beer, lowered the bottle and winked at me. "Come on. You can try to persuade me to give up hamburgers."

I hesitated. He held out his hand, and I took it and followed him downstairs.

seven

I couldn't believe I was sitting right beside Jax. I could only look at him for a couple of seconds at a time— he was too beautiful, and it made me feel all flustered and stupid. I had to take in his face in small glimpses, one feature at a time. Brown eyes that slanted down- ward at the outer corners when he smiled. Thick straight eyebrows. Full lips that could have been a girl's, but didn't look in the least girly on him. I took the joint he held out, inhaled and almost immediately started coughing.

We'd been sitting on a basement couch talking for what felt like hours but was probably only about ten minutes. So far, I'd learned that Jax had moved here from Campbell River, that he had one older brother, that he listened to music that I'd never heard of, and that he used to be really into wrestling but had quit last year.

I hadn't told him much about myself. I was worried I'd say the wrong thing. A couple of times I'd thought he might try to kiss me, but so far he hadn't. I wondered if I'd been imagining things, or misreading them. I couldn't decide if I wanted him to or not.

I'd never actually had an official boyfriend. Things always seemed to get messed up once that friendship line got crossed.

I took another drag on the disappearing joint, feeling the heat on my fingertips where they pinched the paper. "My mom smokes up all the time," I told him, leaning away from him on the couch.

"Your mom?" He laughed. "No way."

"Well, not all the time. Not that much, really, anymore. But she was a total pothead, back when I was a kid."

"Wow. My parents are as straight as they come."

"You're lucky." I passed the joint back to him.

"Nah. They're uptight." Jax took a deep hit, and spoke, still holding the smoke in. "They could use a little chemical help."

"My mother's actually okay with me smoking pot occasionally. She says it's no big deal."

He put his hand over mine and met my eyes. "And your dad?"

"Um, my dad?"

"Yeah. Where does he stand on all that?"

"I don't know," I said. "He lives back east. But…" The words were out of my mouth before I had time to think about them. "He's in town for a visit this week."

"They're divorced, your folks?"

"Something like that."

There was a silence. "Dylan…" Jax cleared his throat. "I did actually know your name, you know."

"You did?"

"I asked someone who you were. Right after that first class I saw you in."

"You did?" I said again.

His hand tightened over mine. "Anyone ever tell you that you've got great eyes?"

"I don't." I dropped my gaze, squirming inside but trying not to show it.

He let go of my hand, put a couple of fingers under my chin and lifted my face so that I had to look at him. "You do. They're a wild color. Kind of turquoise."

"I like brown eyes better," I told him. I could feel myself blushing.

Jax started to lean toward me.

"Hey, you two," a voice said.

I startled and pulled away. "Toni!"

"Sorry." Toni had a big grin on her face. "Bad timing?"

"No, no. It's fine." I was actually sort of relieved. I looked at Jax. "You two know each other, right?"

"I don't think we've actually met." Jax didn't bother to introduce himself.

Nor did Toni. "Look, Dylan, we should head out," she said. "You're supposed to be home by one, right?"

"Technically, but it's sort of flexible." I looked at my watch. Almost two. "Jeez. Not that flexible." I looked at Jax, feeling confused. "I guess I'll see you at school."

"Maybe we can get together sometime this week." He reached for his phone. "Unless you're too busy. With your dad visiting, I mean."

Toni stared. "Your dad visiting," she echoed.

I shot her a look, silently begging her not to say anything. Jax and I exchanged numbers. Then I followed Toni upstairs and out of the house into the cold night air.

"What the hell?" Toni asked. "Your dad visiting? What was that about?"

I felt a little sick and wished I hadn't had those coolers. Or the pot. Or the beer.

"If you didn't want to see Jax, you could have just said so. You didn't need to make up some bullshit excuse." Toni watched me. "But I thought you had a crush on him."

"I did. I do." I shook my head. "I wasn't exactly making it up. I mean, I don't know why I said it. But the thing is, he called. Sperm-donor guy."

Toni stared. "You're kidding. When?"

"Um, yesterday morning? But Mom just told me last night."

There was a long, heavy pause. "Why didn't you tell me?" Toni finally asked.

"I don't know. I wanted to, sort of. It's just hard to talk about it."

"Didn't seem like you had any trouble talking about it with Jax."

I felt a wave of guilt, followed almost immediately by a flicker of defensive anger. I wouldn't have been talking to Jax if she hadn't taken off with Finn the way she always did. I opened my mouth and closed it again. I didn't want to fight with Toni. We never used to fight, but lately it seemed we were often teetering on the brink of an argument.

Toni zipped up her hoodie and shoved her hands in her pockets. "I can't believe that you've known about this since yesterday and didn't even tell me. And then you go and tell a guy you hardly even know."

"I don't know why I did that." I could hear my voice echoing in my head. *He's coming out to visit this week.*

The words had just come spilling out. Did that mean I'd decided to meet him?

I looked at Toni's face. She looked hurt, not angry. "Toni. I told Jax my dad was coming. My *dad*. I mean, I've never thought of him that way. But I guess, you know, he is. Right?"

"Sure. I guess, in the biological sense."

"I have to tell my mom if I want to meet him or not."

We looked at each other for a long moment. When Toni answered, her voice was slow and careful. "What are you going to do?"

I looked away, down the wide street, past all the old houses with their faded paint, past the treed lawns and the crooked fences. I wondered where Mark lived now, whether he was still in Ontario. I hadn't asked Mom. "If I say no, I might never hear from him again."

"So, you'll meet him?"

Over Toni's shoulder, a slender crescent moon shone through thin streaky clouds. It seemed so precarious, suspended in space like that. One big meteor could take it right out and we'd have tidal waves, floods and god knew what else. The human race would be history. I swallowed hard and felt a familiar sharp ache in my throat. "Yeah," I said. "I guess I will."

eIGHT

I woke up feeling tired and heavy, as if gravity had doubled overnight. I dragged myself out of bed and stumbled downstairs. I was hungover from those awful blue coolers. Probably the dye and the chemicals as much as the alcohol.

Karma was sitting on the couch doing homework. She looked up as I entered the room and widened her eyes. "You were way late last night. Amanda's mad."

I could hear Mom banging pots around in the kitchen. "What's she doing in there?"

"Trying to wake you up, I guess."

I made a face. "Passive-aggressive."

Karma shrugged.

I hadn't got home until after two, which was well past the agreed-upon time. Mom didn't call it a curfew—too military, she said. Still, I knew she'd be pissed off. I stepped into the kitchen and watched her pour coffee beans into the grinder and switch it on.

"If you're trying to wake me, I'm already up."

She took her finger off the coffee-grinder button and raised her eyebrows. "Well, not even nine o'clock and look at you. Did you just decide it was so late that you might as well stay up?"

"I couldn't sleep anymore."

"Are you all right? Did something happen at the party?"

"No. I was just thinking about Mark. You know. I think I should meet him."

Her face froze, lips slightly parted, eyes wide, and for a second she looked almost scared. She turned away from me, grinding the coffee beans for a few seconds before responding. "Are you sure you want to do that?" she asked, her back still turned, her voice level.

"Yeah. I'm sure." I stared at her. "You don't want me to, do you? Why not?"

"It's entirely up to you."

Liar. It was so obvious she was hoping I'd decide not to. Well, too bad. She'd never been willing to tell me anything about him. I let out a long shaky breath. "Well, okay. I guess I should call him."

Mom poured the coffee into the filter before realizing it wasn't completely ground. She swore under her breath and started spooning it back out again. "It's up to you, like I said. But…honestly, Dylan, are you sure you want to do this?"

I nodded.

"I'll call him," she said. "Let me talk to him first."

"Okay, but I want to meet him on my own."

"You do? Why?" She still wasn't looking at me.

"Just do. Can you call him now? Please?"

The phone rang. I hesitated, looking at Mom, wondering if she was thinking the same thing—Mark? She picked it up. "Hello?"

I waited impatiently.

"It's Scott," she mouthed. She turned away from me and spoke into the phone. "How's it going?"

I stood there for a moment and watched in disbelief as Mom went on casually chatting as if we hadn't been about to make practically the most important phone call of my entire life. Then I ran up to my room and banged the door closed behind me.

I didn't see why I had to wait for my mom to call Mark. Besides, what if she talked to him first and decided not to let me meet him? He was *my* father, after all. I was the one he wanted to see. I'd call him myself if I knew where he was.

MW, Ocean Front Inn, 214. Mom's little note in her sketchbook. It had to be him. I'd put money on it. I could just pick up the phone and…

What would I say though? What if he didn't know who I was and I had to explain? Should I say I was his daughter? Or was that…presumptuous? He might not think of me that way. Maybe I should just say I was Amanda's daughter.

I looked up the Ocean Front Inn and stared at the phone number on the screen for a long minute. Finally I picked up my cell phone and managed to dial the first three digits before I lost my nerve and pressed End. Maybe I should just wait and let Mom do it after all. I eyed my closed bedroom door. Two minutes, I decided. I'd let fate decide. If Mom was off the phone, I'd go downstairs and let her call. But if Mom was still on the phone in two minutes, I'd call him myself.

Two minutes passed slowly, and my anxiety kept building. I wished I'd said five minutes, but it was too late to change it now. I didn't know why I made up all these stupid bargains with myself, but I couldn't help it. It was something I'd always done.

One of my earliest memories was being in the backseat of the car and counting telephone poles as they flashed past, telling myself that if I counted a hundred poles before we got home, the world wouldn't end before I grew up. I mean, I know that made no sense. I think I even knew it at the time, even though I was only a little kid. But the reason I remembered it so clearly was that it felt so real and so true, and when we pulled into our driveway after only ninety-two poles, I was a mess. The world was going to end and it was my fault.

I guess most kids do stuff like that. I'd just never outgrown it.

When two minutes were up, I opened my door and listened. Amanda's laughter echoed up the stairs. Still on the phone with Scott. I picked up my cell and dialed the number. A man answered and quickly transferred the call to room 214. Mark's room. No questions. Somehow I had almost expected to be asked who I was or what I wanted. The phone rang again, and I held my breath.

"Hello?"

"Is that Mark?"

His voice was guarded. "Yes, it is."

My heart was beating so hard I could feel it in my head, the pulse pounding at my temples. "This is Dylan," I said. "Amanda Jarvis is my mother."

There was a long pause. Then Mark spoke. "I'm so glad to hear from you."

He sounded like a movie actor—sort of relaxed and yet very clear, every word perfectly enunciated. I could hear the smile in his voice. Something else too, some emotion I couldn't identify. Relief, maybe? I let out a long breath and relaxed my fingers on the phone. "I was glad you called. I would really like to meet you."

"Great. That's wonderful."

My bedroom door opened. "Dylan?" Mom looked at me, eyebrows arched questioningly.

"Just a moment," I told Mark. I put my hand over the phone and turned toward her. "I called him."

Her face went chalk-white. She slowly lowered herself to sit on the edge of my bed.

"Dylan?" Mark was saying. "Can I speak to your mother? Is she there?"

I hesitated, feeling an odd reluctance to hand the phone over. I didn't want my mother taking charge, didn't like the reminder that she and Mark had this connection to each other—this relationship, this past—that excluded me. I tried to keep my voice level. "Sure. She's right here." I handed the phone to my mother and stood there listening while the two of them talked.

"Hi…yes…well, that's what Dylan wants, so I suppose… Dinner?" Mom broke off, frowning. "Just a minute." She stood and walked out of the room, taking my phone with her.

"Mom!" I followed her.

She put her hand over the phone. "I'd like some privacy." She stepped into her bedroom and closed the door.

I sat down on the hallway floor. All I could hear was an occasional murmur.

Finally the door opened, and Mom stepped out in to the hall. When she spoke, her voice was as brittle as autumn leaves. "Well, we're meeting him tonight at the hotel. For dinner."

"Tonight?"

"He's only here for a few days. Some conference."

"I said I wanted to see him on my own."

Mom nodded. "I know, I know. But he said he wanted to have us both there."

I scowled. Mark and Mom would probably have some big gosh-it's-so-good-to-see-you-again conversation and start talking about all their old friends. Though maybe not, since she didn't seem exactly happy to hear from him. "Why both of us?"

"He said he wanted to ask you something."

"Ask me what?"

"How the hell would I know?" She shook her head, as if she was taking back the harsh words. "He said he wanted to wait until he saw us."

I rubbed one ankle with my other foot. My big toe was poking out of a hole in my sock. Maybe he wanted to spend some time with me, to get to know me. "Do you think he might want to invite me back to Ontario with him? For a visit?"

"Would you want to go?"

I studied the hole in my sock. "Would you let me?"

She hesitated. "Let's cross that bridge when we come to it."

"Mom? What was he like back then?"

"Oh, Dylan. It was so long ago."

"Yeah, but you've never told me much about him."

"I've shown you a picture."

"I know, but still. Obviously you knew him pretty well, well enough to—you know."

"I didn't know him as well as I thought," she said.

I wondered why she never wanted to talk about him. "Well," I said, watching her face carefully. "You *slept* with him."

She shrugged. "We were kids, Dylan. I was *sixteen*, for god's sake. Your age. Anyway, you'll meet him yourself in a few hours."

I flopped onto my bed and watched her walk out the door. Tonight. I'd actually meet him tonight. My *father*. It was so strange—Mom never called him that; she always just said "Mark." But these last few days, ever since his phone call, I kept catching myself thinking of him in that way.

I stared up at the ceiling. I could see dead flies through the white glass of the lampshade. Gross. God knows how long they'd been there.

I wondered if he thought of me as his daughter. Probably not. My mother had always been very clear that Mark had been a casual fling, a one-night stand. The pregnancy had been an accident, and he had never wanted to see me, didn't want to be involved. He'd never paid a penny of child support, that was for sure.

So why did he want to see me now?

nine

Mom pulled into the hotel's underground parking lot, neatly parked the car and turned off the engine. "Ready?"

"Ready as I'm going to be."

Karma glanced at me, her dark eyes narrowed and her expression unreadable. She unbuckled her seat belt and slid out of the car. Mom was checking her hair in the mirror and putting on lip gloss.

I got out of the car and started walking toward the parking lot entrance, a few steps behind Karma.

"Check this place out!" Karma said over her shoulder. She broke into a run and raced ahead, up the hill to the hotel and through the sliding doors into the lobby.

Mom put her arm over my shoulder. "How are you feeling, baby?"

Like I might throw up. I shrugged her arm off. "Fine. I'm going to..." I gestured in the direction Karma had gone, and sped up, breaking into a jog to catch up with her.

"There's no need to be like that," Mom called after me, but I didn't look back.

In the hotel lobby, Karma was staring at some wooden carvings in a glass case. I stood beside her. I was so on edge my teeth were practically chattering. "Hey."

"Hey. Pretty fancy place, huh?" She lowered her voice. "He must be rich to stay here."

"I guess." A tall woman walked past in a pale blue dress and high heels. I glanced at my reflection in the display case. I was totally underdressed in my cords and sweater.

Mom's reflection appeared over my shoulder. She brushed my arm with her fingers and sighed. "Look... I'm sorry I snapped. I know this dinner is a big deal to you."

To her too, it seemed to me. She was checking her reflection in the glass of the display case, turning her head first one way and then the other. Mom was pretty—great smile, perfect skin, long wavy hair, nice figure—but she didn't usually fuss about her appearance. She lived in jeans or cargo pants, tank tops and hoodies—totally casual—but tonight she was wearing one of her wacky dress-up outfits from Julia's thrift store: a short black skirt over black leggings, combat boots, and a low-cut sequined top that showed too many tattoos and too much cleavage. "Quit checking yourself out," I said irritably. "It's not a date, you know."

She looked away from the glass quickly and gave a forced laugh. "Just wondering if he'd think I'd changed much. It's been…"

"Yeah, sixteen years." I scowled. "I've noticed. Anyway, Mom, he's not here to see you."

I saw her flinch, her eyes widening and the skin under them tightening for the briefest of seconds. She forced a smile. "I know he isn't."

"Well then." I had a feeling I'd just hurt her more than I'd meant to and I didn't understand why. I didn't understand my mother at all. "He's seen pictures anyway," I pointed out. "So he knows what you look like." And me too, I thought.

She flushed. "Dylan. Look, about those pictures…"

"What about them?"

She didn't answer right away, and all at once, I knew. "You never sent them. Right? You never sent him a single one."

"Dylan. Listen."

"You lied to me." My voice came out high-pitched and shaky, and I clenched my fists, trying to stay in control. "God, Mom! You're always going on about honesty, blah blah blah, and you're so full of crap." Posing for this year's picture, two days ago, while she knew the whole time that she wasn't going to send it.

Mom was looking at me, her fingertips pressed against her lips, eyes shining with tears. I stared back and felt like she was a stranger. "I can't believe you lied to me about this," I said. "I can't believe you never sent the pictures."

"He didn't deserve them."

"That's not the point! I wanted to send them. I thought you *had* sent them." My eyes prickled with hot tears and I blinked them away angrily. "You had no right to do this."

"Dylan, come on. It's not like he's ever been a father to you."

"At least he was honest," I said. "You *lied* to me. You've lied to me every year. Letting me take those photographs. Telling me you'd send them."

"He probably wouldn't have written back."

"That's not the point!" I balled my hands into tight fists. I'd never hit anyone, ever, but for the first time in my life, I felt like hitting my mother. Grabbing her shoulders and shaking her. I hated her. Lying to me and acting so self-righteous about it. What did she know? Mark was here now, wasn't he? So maybe he'd been thinking about me too.

Karma was staring at us both, wide-eyed and silent. She always got really small and quiet whenever anyone fought. Me and Mom, Mom and her boyfriends.

I turned my back to my mother and spoke directly to Karma. "Come on, Karma. We'd better go find him." I put my arm around her shoulders and steered us toward the restaurant. I hoped Mom wouldn't follow, but of course she did.

"Just the three of you?" asked a young woman.

"We're meeting someone." Mom scanned the restaurant and I followed her gaze. "That's him," she breathed. "Over there. Oh. My. God."

She was staring at a man sitting at a square table by the far wall. He was playing with his water glass, twisting it slowly around, but as we watched him he looked up and his eyes met Mom's. He stood quickly and stepped toward her.

"God," Mom whispered again. "He hasn't changed. Short hair, but otherwise…and he still has the same walk…"

And then he was there, right in front of us. He nodded briefly at my mother before turning to me. He stared for a long moment, his face unreadable. "You must be Dylan. I'm Mark Wheatcroft." He turned to my mother, right hand extended. "Mandy."

"I go by Amanda now." Mom didn't take his hand. She pushed me and Karma forward. "This is Dylan, and this is Karma, my younger daughter."

I shook hands with Mark, trying not to stare, and we walked over to the table and sat down, which was good because my legs had gone all loose and wobbly. Mark made a few polite comments about how great the hotel was and what a beautiful city this was and all that stuff. Mom was really quiet, and when she spoke, she didn't sound like herself at all. Karma kept kicking me under the table, and I did my best to ignore her.

I was sitting beside Mark, but I didn't want to stare at him, so I studied the cutlery on the table and snuck quick peeks.

He looked way older than I had expected. I'd been picturing him the way he looked in the old photo Mom had given me—a teenager, just a couple years older than me—but of course, he was in his thirties now, same as my mother. He looked older than her though, in his suit and all. Like a businessman. I guessed he was probably rich. Mostly what I was noticing was how much he looked like me. I kept checking off features: same thick dark eyebrows, same almond-shaped blue-green eyes, same square chin with a slight cleft—just a faint dent—in the center. Even his earlobes—they were small and kind of attached, just like mine. My skin was lighter though, pale like Mom's. His was more olive and his hair was cut short and graying a little at the temples, but it was roughly the same shade of dark brown as mine. Mom's was brown, too, but a little lighter and more reddish. Of course, she put henna in it, so it was hard to tell what color it really was.

Finally he spoke directly to me. "So you're Dylan." He shook his head as if he couldn't quite believe it. "Bit of an odd situation, isn't it?"

"I guess." Talk about an understatement.

"I'm starving," Karma announced.

We all turned and looked at her and opened our menus with relief. Something safe to talk about. We managed to fill a good five minutes with comments about how delicious everything sounded, and another five debating whether to order the wild salmon with sesame butter or the Thai noodle salad. Mark moved his hands around a lot when he talked and he kept picking up things from the table—a salt shaker, a napkin—and playing with them. I wondered whether he always did that or whether it meant he was as nervous as I was.

The server came and took our orders. I glanced at the menu. "Thai salad."

Mom raised her eyebrows. "That's got chicken in it. Are you eating meat now?"

"Does it?" I frowned at the menu. "Just a salad then, I guess." I couldn't imagine eating anything anyway.

Finally, the server left and there was a long awkward silence. Mom cleared her throat. "So, what do you do these days, Mark?"

"Lawyer." He turned his water glass around, leaving wet rings on the table.

Mom raised her eyebrows. "Just like the old man after all."

Mark laughed, but he sounded uncomfortable. "Well, teenage rebellion is fine, but I couldn't really do construction forever. And you, Amanda?" He shook his head. "Well, I guess I already know that, don't I? You run a cleaning business. That's how I found you. Nice website, by the way."

"I do photography too." Mom sounded defensive.

"You're still into that? Really?"

Mom's voice was a little sharp. "Why not?"

"No, no. That's great, really. I'm impressed." His head tilted, questioning. "So you must be busy. Working, looking after two kids..."

Mom hesitated for a moment, her lips pursed. "Karma is Sheri's daughter. Sheri Russell, remember?"

He nodded. "I know. In fact, that's how I..." He broke off and hesitated for a moment, glancing at my mother. Her eyes were narrowed, lips pale, every muscle tense. He cleared his throat and looked away, turning to face Karma. "I'm so sorry, Karma. Lisa—my wife—we heard about your mother's accident from an old friend. We hadn't seen Sheri in years, but I used to know her well. I was so sad to hear about what happened."

Mom put an arm around Karma's shoulder.

Karma shrugged her off. "You knew my mom? When?"

"Back when I was a teenager." He cleared his throat and looked down at the table. "Back when Sheri wasn't much older than Dylan is now."

"Same age," Mom said. Her voice sounded tight.

Karma just nodded. "Uh-huh. I know Amanda and Mom were best friends in school."

I leaned forward. "So, were you guys all in the same class?"

He shook his head. "I wasn't at school with them. I met your mom a few weeks after I graduated."

I'd always assumed they'd met at school. Actually, I was pretty sure Mom had said so. "So where'd you meet then?"

Mark laughed. "At a party, actually. Someone's backyard." He looked at me, head cocked to one side. "Summer nights, patios, too much beer flowing. You know the scene."

Mom interrupted, her voice hard-edged. "Jesus Christ, Mark. Didn't we agree there was no need to drag up the past?"

So that was why she'd rushed out of my room with the phone—to make Mark promise to adhere to her stupid code of secrecy. I wondered if the photographs weren't the only thing she'd been lying to me about. "I guess Mark is free to talk about whatever he wants," I said coldly.

Mom stared at Mark like she was just daring him to say another word. He shrugged. "Relax, Mandy."

"Amanda." She was silent for a long minute. Then she shook her head. "Sorry. It's fine. So we met at a party. Whatever." She cleared her throat. "All ancient history. So, Mark, do you and Lisa have kids?"

Changing the subject. Like that wasn't totally obvious. I wondered what she was hiding. I mean, I already knew she'd been a total pothead and got pregnant at sixteen from a one-night stand. It wasn't as if she had some perfect straight-A student, moral leader and virgin-till-marriage image to maintain.

"A daughter." Mark pulled out his phone. "Her name's Casey. She's almost four." He looked at the image on the screen for a long moment, his mouth twisted into a crooked smile. I thought he was going to hand the phone to Mom, but he handed it to me instead. "Your half sister," he said.

I took the phone from him and stared at the photo. My half sister. A round-faced girl, smiling, with short dark hair and big eyes. Cute kid, I guess. My stomach was full of something much squirmier than butterflies and my throat was getting all tight. As quickly as I could without being rude, I passed the phone to Mom.

"Must be hard to be away from her," Mom said.

"It is," Mark said. His voice sounded funny, like he really meant it. Like he could hardly stand to be away from his precious little girl.

I sucked on my bottom lip. He'd been away from me, his other daughter, for my whole life and he hadn't cared at all. Hadn't even cared enough to stay in touch with Mom to find out how I was doing.

Mark was fiddling with his napkin, folding it into a small square and unfolding it again.

"How come you got in touch?" I blurted out. "I mean, you never wanted to see me before, so how come you wanted to meet me now?"

He squeezed the bridge of his nose and then rubbed his hands over his cheeks. I could see a faint bluish shadow, like he hadn't shaved that day. He cleared his throat. "It's a complicated situation."

I wondered if his wife knew about me, and I felt a flush of shame, as if I'd done something wrong. "You were embarrassed? Ashamed of me?"

He made a small noise of protest. "Of course not."

Across the table, Karma was wide-eyed, her mouth hanging open slightly.

He picked up his napkin, shook out the wrinkles and folded it neatly in half. "Maybe you should talk to your mother about this."

I raised my eyebrows. "She can't tell me why you never wanted to be involved, can she? So I'm asking you."

There was a long uncomfortable silence. Mark looked at my mother and made a helpless gesture. She just shook her head, lips clamped together tightly. I looked down at the white tablecloth. I wished my mother wasn't sitting there listening, but I had to ask. "Didn't you ever even wonder about me?"

Mark looked at me. "I'm here, now. I know it must seem odd, but can we just move forward? Get to know each other?"

"Kind of hard to get to know you if you can't even answer a simple question," I said.

Mark rubbed his hands over his face again and said nothing. The server arrived and began placing plates of food on the table, all beautifully arranged and decorated with curly bits of finely sliced vegetables. When the server was gone, Mom looked at Mark. "Why are you doing this?" she asked. "We don't need you interfering in our family."

He picked up his napkin, twisted it into a tight ball and let it drop onto the table beside his plate. "Long story," he said. "Let's just enjoy our dinner and get to know each other. Then perhaps the girls could take a little walk and you and I could have a few minutes alone together. There's something I'd like to discuss with you."

My heart fluttered. He was going to ask me to come and visit, maybe even stay for a while. That had to be it. What else could it be?

ten

Dinner was painful. I just wanted to know what Mark was doing here, and I guess Mom did too. I wished he'd get on with it. I poked at my salad, sliding tomato and cucumber slices to one side and twirling shredded carrots with my fork.

"Beautiful city," Mark said.

It was at least the third time we'd covered that particular topic.

Mom nodded. "Yes."

Long silence. I chewed on a piece of lettuce that tasted like nothing at all and waited for Mark to say how nice the hotel was.

"It's a lovely hotel," Mark said.

Mom shrugged. "I wouldn't know."

Another long silence.

"So, did Lisa come with you?" Mom asked at last.

Mark shook his head. "She stayed with our daughter." His eyes flickered toward me and back to Mom. "With Casey."

"Of course. So. Is she working, or…"

"Not right now. She's a full-time parent."

"And you have a full-time income. Must be nice," Mom said.

Mark just shook his head and didn't say anything.

I didn't see why she had to be bitchy about it. It wasn't Mark's fault that no one wanted to buy her weird photographs. Maybe she was pissed off to find out he was so wealthy. After all, he'd never paid a penny of child support. I wondered if that would change now, since he'd finally decided to meet me.

Still, I couldn't help noticing that Mark wasn't asking me anything. If he was here because he wanted to get to know me, you'd think he'd show some interest. I pushed my plate away. "I'm not really hungry. Um, Karma?"

She stuck another French fry into her mouth. "What?"

"Ready to go for a walk?"

She looked at her plate. "No."

"Come on…" I kicked her gently under the table.

She looked up at me.

I mouthed, "Please?"

Karma sighed, casting a final regretful look at her unfinished hamburger. "Okay. Okay."

❧

Karma wandered around, but I stayed close to the restaurant entrance, hidden behind a giant potted palm tree, watching Mom and Mark. I wished I could hear their conversation, but they were a good thirty or forty feet away with several tables of chattering people between us.

Mom was leaning toward him. I could imagine what she was saying. She'd be telling him to get on with it, spit it out, say why he was here.

Mark put his elbows on the table and rested his chin on his knuckles.

Mom folded her hands in her lap.

He was talking. Talking. Talking.

Then Mom suddenly tensed. She raised her voice, but I couldn't hear the words. She started to stand, and Mark grabbed her arm.

Mom sank back into her seat and he let go of her wrist, leaning toward her.

I couldn't imagine what they could be talking about. Maybe he wanted me to visit and Mom was saying no. Or…

Stone, I told myself. *Be as hard as stone. Be ice. Don't let yourself care.* I swallowed hard and my throat was so tight it felt like I was swallowing marbles. Even if Mark wanted me to visit, I wasn't sure I would. He hadn't ever wanted to meet me before. Why should he get what he wanted now?

A man at the table closest to the entrance stood up, blocking my view. Karma sidled up to me.

"What's going on?"

"I don't know. It looked like they were fighting, but I couldn't hear anything." I leaned to one side, trying to see them without being obvious. A waitress standing just inside the entrance gave me an odd look. I ignored her. The man sat back down, but I couldn't even see Mom's and Mark's faces—just their heads bent low over the table in conversation.

"What do you think of him?" Karma asked. "Do you like him?"

I shrugged.

"He looks like you, don't you think?"

"I guess. Sort of. I mean, for a middle-aged man."

"I think he looks like a movie star," Karma said.

I snorted. "He looks like a middle-aged lawyer, which is what he is."

She shook her head impatiently. "Like that guy, what's his name? In that movie where the girl gets kidnapped and—"

"Shut up a minute," I told her. Mom had just pushed her chair back from the table and stood up. "I wonder what they're talking about."

"Old times, I bet," Karma said. "I wonder if he was ever *my* mom's boyfriend. Then he'd sort of be like my dad too."

"Oh, Karma..." I looked at her, wondering what to say. Most of the time she was such a tough, scrappy little kid and then she'd come out with something like this, and I'd feel so sad for her. I'd remember that she was really an orphan, just like in all the old-fashioned kids' books I used to read—Mary in the *Secret Garden,* Anne in *Anne of Green Gables,* Sara Crewe in *The Little Princess.* Though of course in the end Sara turned out not to be an orphan after all. I opened my mouth to say something lame about how it was okay just being the three of us, her and me and Mom—but next thing I knew, Mom came flying out of the restaurant. She grabbed both me and Karma. "Let's go."

She hustled us across the lobby, and out through the automatic doors. I pulled free. "Mom! What's wrong?"

She didn't answer. A soft rain was falling. I started to cry. "Stop it, Mom. You can't do this. Just tell me what happened, okay?"

Mom just pressed her lips tightly together and shook her head. She kept walking, down the hill and into the underground parking lot. "Not now, Dylan. Get in the car."

"Mom!"

"Don't argue, Dylan." She was almost shouting. I didn't think I'd ever seen her so upset. "You too, Karma."

Karma got in the car, her eyes wide and scared. I hesitated. "Please...can't I just run back and say goodbye?"

Mom banged the palms of her hands against the car roof. "Get in the goddamn car, Dylan."

I got in and slammed the door behind me so hard the jolt made my whole arm ache. Mom reversed out of the parking spot, swore as she almost hit the back of a pickup truck and drove quickly out of the parking garage. I stared out the car window, twisting around to watch the hotel disappear behind us.

What the hell was her problem? It didn't make sense. I couldn't even imagine what Mark could have said or done to make Mom walk out like that. She'd already practically agreed that I could go to Ontario to visit. I opened my mouth to beg for an explanation, but something—some fear—stopped me. What if it was something really bad? For all I knew, Mark could've spent the last ten years in jail for child molestation or murder or something. Maybe he had just told my mother something horrible. Something I would rather not know.

I pushed my knuckles against the sharp edge of my teeth and closed my eyes so tightly it hurt. I could feel hot tears squeezing out anyway. Karma's small warm hand touched mine. A tentative touch, a firmer grasp, a long squeeze. I squeezed back gratefully, but after a minute,

I pulled away. Karma knew how it felt to lose a real parent. What had I lost? Nothing.

The drive home was long and silent. It was still raining, a steady *tap-splatter-tap* against the windshield. The wipers squeaked and the one on the passenger side left a wide swath of window unwiped. I felt myself retreating further and further inside. Like one of those Russian dolls. Like a snail. I wished I could just curl up inside a shell and be left alone.

When we had pulled into the driveway, my mother turned off the engine but didn't get out of the car. Without turning to look at us, she spoke. "Listen...."

I froze, one hand on the door handle, not sure whether I wanted to hear what she had to say.

"I'm sorry I dragged you two out of there like that," she said, her words coming out slow and careful, like she'd spent the drive planning exactly what she would say. "The thing is, I don't think Mark is someone that we want in our lives."

I stared at my hands. My nails had a scattering of white marks across them, like tiny little scars. "Why?" My voice was a hoarse whisper. "What did he say?"

She shook her head. "As your mother, it is my job to make the decisions that I think are best for you—"

I cut her off, anger starting to build inside me like static electricity. I could feel the tiny hairs on my arms lifting.

"Since when?" I said. "Since when do you base your decisions on what's best for us?"

"Dylan…"

"No, really. Because it seems to me that it's always all about you and what you want." I would have said more, but beside me, Karma was starting to cry silently, tears welling up and spilling over. She wiped them away fiercely when she saw me looking, and turned to face the window.

Mom shook her head. "He's a selfish asshole. He always was." She looked at me, and then looked away, blinking. Her eyes were wet. "Just do your best to forget about him, Dylan. Please."

‚Äî

"She wouldn't even give you an explanation?" Toni asked. She scrunched her nose and wrinkled her forehead like this was the weirdest thing she'd ever heard.

It was Monday morning and we were standing in the school hallway. People were rushing past, voices raised, laughter ringing out, locker doors banging. I focused on Toni's round freckled face and wished I'd never told anyone that Mark was here. Then I wouldn't look like such an idiot. I wouldn't have to listen to all these questions. I didn't have any answers to give anyway. "No. She said I should forget about him."

"Huh." Toni was silent for a moment. "I bet he made a pass at her. You think?"

"Nah. He's married."

"So? Didn't stop my dad," Toni said bitterly.

Toni's dad had taken off after he got reacquainted with his high-school girlfriend at a twenty-year reunion. "I don't think so," I said flatly. "Anyway, my mom never gets mad if someone makes a pass at her. She loves it when guys flirt with her." I rolled my eyes. "She says it's a compliment."

"Speaking of which…" Toni raised her eyebrows. "What's up with you and Jax?"

"Nothing."

"Yeah? That's not how it looked at Jessica's."

I shrugged. "Yeah. I don't know."

"Mmm." Toni glanced at her watch. "Look, I should go. I told Finn I'd meet him at lunch." She shifted from one foot to the other. "You don't mind, do you?"

"I'm used to it," I said, and instantly regretted it. The words had just slipped out.

"What does that mean?"

"Just that whenever Finn is around, I get dumped. Okay? That's all."

Toni's eyes darkened. "That's not fair."

"Whatever." I knew it wasn't fair, but right now I didn't care. The anger inside me felt like a living thing, something I could barely control. It wasn't even Toni I was mad at, but that didn't matter either.

She looked annoyed. "You don't understand, Dylan. I mean, you've never even had a boyfriend."

"Fuck you," I said. As soon as I'd said it, my anger vanished. I wanted to snatch the words back. I didn't think I'd ever said that before, to anyone.

Her eyes widened and she flinched as if I had tried to hit her.

I couldn't think of anything else to say. I just stood there stupidly, like a bystander watching some other version of myself, some robot-clone gone berserk. Dylan Jarvis Version Two, maybe. DJ 2.0. My new alter ego.

Toni took off, half running down the hall. We'd never had a fight like this before. I waited to feel upset or angry, but all I felt was kind of hollow and detached.

I was still standing there, staring down the empty hall, when Jax walked up.

"Hey," he said.

"Hi," I said.

"What're you up to?"

"Nothing." I felt oddly confident. I could look right at him, no trouble. Maybe DJ 2.0 was still in charge.

"Wanna come for a bike ride?"

"A bike ride?"

"Motorbike." He raised one eyebrow, daring me. "Come on. Just a quick spin."

"I've got class."

He raised one eyebrow.

My heart was beating fast. "Do you have an extra helmet?"

"Of course I do." He laughed. "What are you, Safety Girl?"

"Just checking."

"Don't worry," Jax said, winking. "I always take precautions."

I blushed. Was he talking about what I thought he was? I summoned DJ 2.0 back. Let her deal with this. "Okay," I heard myself saying. "I'll come for a ride."

❦

I was terrified for the first few minutes, convinced we were going to crash any second, imagining my body lying under a twisted heap of smoking metal, legs torn and bleeding, neck snapped, spinal cord severed. But after a while, when nothing remotely like that had happened, I began to relax. My arms were wrapped around Jax's waist, and the engine was too loud for conversation.

To be this close to him, physically, our bodies actu-ally touching, and yet not have to worry about talking or moving or even about making eye contact…it was perfect. I could feel my heart beating over the thrum of the motorbike's engine. The wind was forcing tears from my eyes and chasing them across my temples and into my hair.

I could have driven all day, but eventually Jax pulled the bike off the side of the road and onto a grassy verge. He shut off the engine and I let go of him, feeling suddenly awkward.

He twisted around to face me, grinning widely. "So? What did you think?"

"I loved it," I said. "It was incredible. I didn't know…"

"Yeah. It's better than anything." He winked. "Well, almost anything."

And I, Dylan Jarvis—shy Dylan, uptight-about-sex Dylan, never-had-a-boyfriend Dylan—just laughed. I felt like I was high.

Jax took his helmet off and shook his hair back from his face. "So what did you do for the rest of the weekend? Anything interesting?"

To my surprise, I found myself spilling the whole story. It was like running downhill. I talked faster and faster and once I got started, I couldn't stop.

"Shit," Jax said when I finally ran out of words. "That's wild. So your dad's this total mystery man. That's wild."

I didn't see what was so wild about it, but I just shrugged. "I guess."

"So why do you figure your mom won't tell you what's going on? Don't you want to know?"

I thought about it for a moment. Did I really want to know? "Yeah," I said. "Even if he's…you know, a criminal or something…I want to know."

"So, you gotta find out."

I shook my head. "My mother won't tell me. When she makes up her mind about something…"

"Yeah, your mom sounds like a bitch. Why don't you just ask him yourself?"

Bitch. The word startled me and I felt a flicker of loyalty toward my mother, but it was almost immediately wiped out by another wave of anger. What right did Mom have to keep information from me? She was always going on about how close we were. Right. I knew which of her boyfriends had given her an STD and I knew about the time she got busted for driving drunk, but I knew next to nothing about my own father. And she'd lied to me about sending those photographs. For eight *years*. I wondered what else she'd lied to me about.

I'd had enough. If my mother wouldn't tell me, maybe Mark would.

eleven

After school, I was supposed to take Karma to the Boys and Girls Club. Mom had signed her up for another group, and I figured I could drop her off and then, if I had enough nerve, go down to the Ocean Front Hotel and see if Mark was still there. Mom thought I was having dinner at Toni's place, so she wouldn't worry if I was late getting home.

"The last after-school club was okay because Scott was there," Karma told me as we got on the bus. "But the woman running this one is really annoying."

"How come?" My hands were sweating just thinking about my plan. I pressed them against my jeans and hoped I wouldn't lose my nerve.

Karma shrugged. "She just bugs me. She's pretends we're just playing games, but she's always trying to get us to talk about stuff. About our *feelings*." She made it sound like a bad word.

"Did you tell Mom you don't want to go?"

"Duh. Course I did." She slid into a back-row seat. "Last week I went downtown instead. That's why Amanda made you go with me today, you know. To make sure I got there."

"You skipped your group?" I sat down beside her, not sure whether to be impressed or concerned. Even I knew that hanging out downtown was a shortcut to all kinds of trouble for a kid her age.

She nodded. "It's a waste of time. Anyway, I wanted to look at the bike repair stuff down at Green City Cycle."

I laughed. "Of course you did."

"What's so funny?"

"Nothing." I pushed the button. "Your stop. You want me to meet you after or can you make your own way home?"

Karma didn't budge. "What are you going to do? Are you meeting Toni?"

"MYOB, kiddo."

"Dylan…tell me." The bus pulled to a stop, but Karma didn't budge. "Please?"

I watched a couple of passengers swipe bus passes. "If I tell you, will you get off the bus?"

"Sure." She stood up.

An older man sat down across the aisle from us, and I lowered my voice, even though no one was listening. "I'm going to see if I can find Mark."

Karma's eyes widened. "As in, your father?" She sat back down. "I'm totally coming with you."

"Karma!"

She didn't budge. The bus driver pulled back into the flow of traffic, heading toward downtown. "Mom's going to kill me," I said.

"Because of me skipping group or you seeing Mark?"

"Either. Both. Take your pick."

Karma grinned. "I won't tell if you don't."

"The Club will call her and you know it." I just hoped Mark wouldn't do the same.

"Are you mad?" Karma sounded more curious than worried.

"You drive me crazy, you know that?"

"I know."

"No, I'm not mad." I was actually kind of glad of the company, and now that I'd told Karma what I was doing, I was less likely to chicken out.

"I'd do the same thing, if it was my dad," Karma said. "I wonder why Amanda made us leave like that. You think he said something that made her flip out?"

I shook my head. "No clue."

"Maybe he wants custody or something. He's a lawyer, right?"

"Seems a bit unlikely. I'm too old for that, don't you think? Anyway, he hasn't even wanted to see me until now." What the hell was I doing? My mother would murder me if she found out. Maybe I could ask Mark not to tell her. If he was even still here. Maybe he'd gone home already. Maybe I'd never see him again. My thoughts were spiraling out of control. *Polar ice melting,* I told myself. *South Pacific islands being slowly submerged. Tsunamis. Bee colonies collapsing. Global food shortages.* It didn't work. It didn't put my own worries into perspective or help my panic to subside. Even if the world was on the brink of catastrophe, I still wanted to see Mark. Even if he turned out to be a drug dealer or a child molester, I still wanted to know why he had come.

We rode in silence the rest of the way, and when we finally got off the bus, my legs felt shaky. Karma slipped her small brown hand into mine, and I made a face at her as we walked toward the hotel.

"Changed your mind?" she asked.

"No. We're here now. Anyway, I want to see him. I'm just nervous."

"Want me to come in with you? Or should I wait out here?"

I hesitated. I could use the moral support, but what if Mark told me something I didn't want her to hear? "Wait out here. If you don't mind?"

She shook her head and plopped down on a sidewalk bench. "That's okay. I've got a book."

I walked up the curving driveway, through the revolving doors, and up to the reception desk. "Is Mark Wheatcroft still staying here? Can you call him and tell him Dylan is here to see him?"

The woman—round-faced and as freckled as Toni— smiled, nodded and dialed Mark's room number. I held my breath. What if he'd already left? But the hotel staff would know that, wouldn't they? They wouldn't call his room if he'd checked out.

"Hello, Mr. Wheatcroft?" the woman said. "Um, Dylan is downstairs in the lobby?" She made it sound like a question.

I watched her face carefully, trying to read Mark's response in her expression.

The woman smiled at me and smoothed her fair hair with one hand. "Have a seat. He said he'd be right down."

"Thanks." I wandered over to the display case that Karma had been looking at the night before and stared at the carvings. I wondered if Mark would be angry that I'd come on my own. *Just forget about him,* Mom had said. As if I could.

Finally the elevator doors opened and Mark stepped out.

"Dylan." He smiled widely. "I'm so glad to see you. I knew Amanda would come around once she'd had time to think about it." He looked around the lobby. "Where is she?"

I shook my head. "I came on my own."

"Oh." He looked confused. "But…she did tell you?"

My heart was pounding hard and fast. "She didn't tell me anything."

Mark's face fell. "So you're not here because…"

"I'm here because I want to know what's going on." My voice was shaking and my eyes were suddenly wet. I brushed the back of my hand across them quickly.

"Oh." Mark frowned. "I should probably call your mother."

"Don't."

We stared at each other for a moment. A muscle in Mark's jaw was twitching.

I wondered if he ground his teeth like I did. I used to wear a tooth guard at night so I wouldn't wear my teeth down to stubs. I watched him making up his mind. Finally he nodded decisively and gestured to the doors.

"Let's go for a walk, okay? And I'll tell you what's going on."

꩜

It had clouded over. The sky was a thick damp gray streaked with dirty white clouds. I could see Karma's small figure, her back to me, still sitting on the sidewalk bench, and I wished for a second that I'd told her to come with me. Not for her sake—she never minded being alone—but for my own. I'd feel better if I was still holding her hand. I clenched my fists inside my pockets and followed Mark in the opposite direction, away from the street and along a paved path down near the harbor. A cool breeze blew off the water, and I shivered, tucking my hands into my sleeves and pulling my hoodie around myself more tightly. A harbor ferry chugged slowly toward the inner harbor. A sailboat scudded by, its canvas white against the dark green-gray of the waves.

I snuck a glance at Mark as we walked. He was wearing a long black coat over dark gray pants, and I thought about how he lived in a different world from me and Mom and Karma. A world where you didn't have to worry about paying the rent. He and Lisa probably lived somewhere nice, in a big house they owned. I wondered what he thought about Mom cleaning houses for a living. He and Lisa probably paid someone like Mom to keep their own place clean.

"It's beautiful here," Mark said.

"Yeah. We've already covered that topic pretty thoroughly." I knew it was rude, but if I had to make more small talk, my head was going to explode.

He sighed. "Look, I don't know what the right thing to do is. I know you want an explanation, but I'm sure you also realize your mother is not going to be happy about this. About me talking to you."

I waited.

"Okay. The thing is, I think you have a right to make up your own mind. If I was sure that Amanda would tell you herself, I wouldn't say anything."

He was trying to convince himself that he was doing the right thing, I realized. I nodded, wanting to help him along. "Sure. That makes sense."

Mark stopped walking and turned to face me. "Dylan, what I'm about to tell you…just promise me you'll think about it, okay? Even if you're upset. Promise me you'll really think about it."

I nodded, confused. "Sure. I promise."

He tilted his head to one side, studying me as if I was a puzzle of some kind. "My daughter, Casey," he said slowly. "I showed you her picture last night."

"I remember." That big-eyed girl he'd called my half sister.

"Casey has something called acute lymphoblastic leukemia." Mark was speaking slowly and carefully, watching my face. "It's a blood disease—a kind of cancer of the blood cells."

"Jeez. That's awful. I'm sorry." I wondered if she was dying. It wasn't the kind of question you could ask. Besides, what if the answer was yes? I wouldn't know what to say.

"Yes. It is awful." He cleared his throat. "She was a healthy kid until last winter. Around Christmas she started losing weight, getting ear infections and sore throats and saying she was tired all the time. She'd had a bad flu, and we figured she was just run-down. Then she started complaining of leg pain, and Lisa—my wife— took her to the doctor. They did blood tests." He shook his head, like he was still having trouble believing it.

I pushed the toe of my runner against the soft grass at the edge of the path and wondered what all this had to do with me.

"She had chemo, which was hell. But it seemed like it worked. She went into remission and we thought we'd beaten it, but this fall she relapsed. We almost lost her. We got a second remission, but the doctors say it won't last. She needs a bone marrow transplant. Lisa and I were both tested, of course, but neither of us were a match. Lisa wanted to do *in vitro* fertilization, to try to have another child who could be a donor, but she had a lot of complications with her last pregnancy and, well, we didn't know how much time we had. And then…" He cleared his throat. "Then I thought of you."

"That's a first," I said.

"You don't understand. Mandy has put me in an impossible…" He shook his head, frowning. "Never mind that for now." He reached out and took my hand. "Listen. Casey's best chance of survival is if we can find a donor who's a good match. You're her half sister. It's a long shot, but I came out here to ask if you would consider being tested."

I pulled my hand away. I felt like one of those snow globes—like someone had picked me up and turned me upside down and given me a hard shake. All of my thoughts and feelings were whirling and floating around inside. I shook my head.

Mark misunderstood. "Don't answer now." He leaned toward me, his eyes intense, locked on mine. "You promised you'd think about it."

"I have to go," I said numbly.

"But you will think about it?" He grabbed my arm.

I looked down at his wrist. His sleeve had pulled back a couple of inches and a glimpse of color flashed. I stared at it. A tattoo. A hummingbird tattoo.

"I'm sorry." Mark let go and stepped back. "I fly back east on Thursday," he said. He fumbled in his pocket and handed me a card. "Call me on my cell. Here or at home."

"You have the same tattoo as Mom."

"Crazy thing to do," he said, shaking his head. "It wasn't as if hummingbirds had any great meaning to us either.

We just flipped through the book and picked a picture we liked. Could have been worse, I guess. At least we didn't get skulls. Or each other's names."

I took the card. "I have to go," I said again. Then I turned and ran back up the grassy slope toward the hotel, eyes stinging, tears cold on my cheeks.

"Hey, Dylan." Karma grabbed my shoulder. Her eyes were wide and scared. "You just ran right past me. What's wrong? What happened?"

I shook my head. "Nothing."

"If he hurt you…" She looked ready to find Mark and kill him if necessary.

"No. No, nothing like that."

Karma's voice wobbled slightly, as if she might start to cry. "After you went off with him, I started freaking out and thinking, like, what if he's a pervert or something?"

"He's not."

"But you don't want to talk about it?"

"I just want to go home," I said.

This was the worst part, the most shameful thing: the first thought I'd had when Mark had said Casey was sick was that maybe if Casey wasn't around, he'd see me as a daughter instead. It was a horrible, sick, twisted thought to have. I hated myself for having that thought. And anyone else who knew it would hate me too. Even Karma.

Karma rode the bus halfway home with me and hopped off at the Boys and Girls Club.

"I'll just apologize for being late. That way I miss most of the group and they won't call Amanda," she said. "Are you going to be okay?"

"Yeah." Karma looked worried, so I tried to grin at her. "Go on. I'll be fine."

She gave my arm a funny little pat and got off the bus, and I rode it the rest of the way home. I couldn't believe Mom hadn't told me why he was here. By the time I was kicking off my shoes in our front hall and walking up the stairs, I still hadn't decided whether to talk to her about it or pretend that I didn't know. She'd be furious that I'd gone to see Mark on my own but…

Crap. At the entrance to the living room, I stopped dead. I stood and stared for a moment. Mom and Scott were making out on the couch. There was an open bottle of wine on the table and the living room smelled like pot.

Scott jumped up when he saw me. His shirt was off and his jeans were unbuttoned. I looked away quickly.

"Sorry, sorry," he muttered, presumably doing up his pants. "How are you, Dylan?"

"Fine." *God.* My face was burning.

Mom didn't even bother getting up. She sat up, her shirt halfway unbuttoned, black lace bra showing, and laughed. "You're home early."

"I'm going upstairs," I said flatly.

"Wait, wait. Come here, baby. Come see Scott's new tattoo." Mom grabbed Scott, who was bending to pick up his T-shirt, and held up his arm. "Check it out."

On his left bicep was a freshly inked skeleton drummer, the skin around it reddened and shiny with oil.

"I drew it. What do you think? Nice, huh?"

So that tattoo hadn't been for her at all. I really didn't care anymore. "Are you stoned?"

She giggled again. "Just a bit tipsy. It's Scott's birthday. We were celebrating."

"Whatever." I turned to leave, but Scott beckoned to me.

"Hang on a sec. I brought something for you." He pulled his T-shirt over his head, sat back down on the couch and rummaged in a canvas bag by his feet. "Here. Karma told me you were a committed environmentalist, so I thought, maybe..."

He held out a DVD and I glanced at it. A two-year-old documentary on global warming. "I've already seen it," I told him. Behind him, I could see my mother's face. She knows about Casey, I thought. She knows and she's just partying like always, and she hasn't even bothered to tell me.

"And? What'd you think?" Scott prompted.

"It was okay."

"I just showed it to one of my teen groups." He looked at the cover picture for a moment before dropping it back in his bag. "Good movie, but it'd be more powerful if it went beyond the problem and actually explored solutions."

"Maybe there aren't any," I said. "Maybe we've screwed up the planet so badly that it's too late. Even if we stopped burning fossil fuels completely, right now, the temperature would go on rising for another fifty to a hundred years."

"But isn't that kind of attitude part of the problem?" Scott said.

I rolled my eyes. I wasn't going to listen to this crap. "Oh, please," I said. "Multinational corporations are the problem. Our meat-based North American diet is the problem. Our whole consumption-based disposable society is the problem."

"I'm serious," he said.

"Uh, yeah. So am I."

Mom glared at me and I scowled back. Why should I let her pothead boyfriend give me a lecture?

Scott grinned at me. "Come on. You know how it is. Everyone's like, 'Well what can I do? Look at all the factories and planes belching out carbon gases. I might as well just keep driving my suv and crank up the air con.' So nothing changes."

"This isn't an individual problem," I said. "So individual solutions won't fix it. Anyway, I'm trying to be realistic. Maybe it really is too late."

"So what if it is? We should all just give up? Screw it, everyone just do what you want, too bad about the planet?"

I blinked. "No. Of course not. I just think that maybe even if we do everything we can do, it might not be enough." I thought of Casey. If we couldn't even figure out how to stop one little kid from dying, how the hell could we hope to save a planet?

"I guess that's possible," Scott said.

I shrugged. "Probable." And the other thing that was *probable* was Scott thinking I was a real downer. It was *probable* that he was wondering how someone like Mom ended up with a kid as negative as me.

"Still, even if you are right, we still have to make choices, right? And hope is important."

I wondered if this was how he talked to the kids he worked with, and whether he thought he was being inspiring. I didn't feel inspired, but I had to give him points for effort. "Whatever," I said. "Anyway, I've got homework, so…I'll just…" I gestured down the hall.

"Should be working on a paper for school myself." Scott put his hand on my mother's wrist and rubbed his thumb across the hummingbird tattoo. "Catch you later, Dylan."

Not if I can help it. I dragged my eyes away from the hummingbird and as quickly as I could without actually running, I scooted away and shut myself in my room. *God.* Spare me the bonding session with my mother's half-naked boyfriend.

TWELVE

Mom's hummingbird tattoo was green with a flash of red at its throat, wings spread mid-beat as it hovered forever at her wrist. Because of the sound of my heartbeat *in utero*, she'd said. I'd looked it up once and found out that a hummingbird heart actually beats at about ten times the rate of a fetal heart. But the idea had been nice anyway.

Until I found out that the whole story was just one more lie.

I wondered if she was planning to tell me about Casey or if she was just going to let her die without even giving me a chance to try to help. She was pretty irresponsible sometimes, but I wouldn't have thought she could be that selfish.

I switched on my laptop. Acute something leukemia, he'd said. Acute lymphoblastic leukemia. My fingers flew over the keys and within a few seconds, I had a definition: *Acute lymphoblastic leukemia (ALL) is a form of leukemia, characterized by the overproduction and continuous multiplication of malignant and immature white blood cells (also known as lymphoblasts) in the bone marrow. It could be fatal if left untreated as ALL spreads into the bloodstream and other vital organs quickly. ALL is most common in childhood with a peak incidence at four to five years of age.*

Casey wasn't quite four yet.

Mark's daughter. His real daughter.

My half sister.

I wanted to call Toni and talk to her about it— but there was no way that I could tell anyone. Not unless I knew for sure that I was going to do it. Not unless I was actually going to be a bone marrow donor.

Anyway, I'd told Toni to fuck off. I felt panicky at the memory—what if she hated me?—and pushed the thought away.

I typed in *bone marrow donation*, clicked onto a Canadian Blood Services site and started reading. *The donor is usually admitted to the hospital early on the morning of the harvest date...general anesthetic...marrow is withdrawn from the donor's hip bones using a special syringe and needle in the operating room...*I pressed my hands against my hip bones and tried to imagine a doctor sticking needles into their sharp ridges. My mouth was desert-dry and I felt sick. It was all just so...humiliating. I'd been so quick to assume Mark wanted to get to know me. But he didn't care about me at all. He just wanted my bone marrow.

*The donor can generally go home the same day but may experience some temporary soreness in the area...*I pushed my chair back from the computer, heart pounding, and sat staring out the window. The sun was low in the late afternoon sky, shining weakly through a crack in the clouds. There was a weird greenish glow in the east. I wondered if it was because of all the pollution.

When we were kids, Toni and I used to design cities that people could live in after the air got too polluted to breathe—whole communities inside great glass domes, or under the sea, crowded together like a colony of ants. Back then, I'd had a lot of faith in people's ability to pull together to cope with change. I hadn't realized that people were basically selfish. Me. Mom. Mark.

Everyone was just looking out for themselves.

⟨❀⟩

I managed to avoid Mom until dinnertime, when I had to go and sit at the table with her. The knots in my stomach twisted a little tighter every time I thought about all the lies and secrets. Mom had actually cooked dinner for once, but it was hard to eat.

I chewed a mouthful of rice and listened to the sound of Vital Shrines, Scott's former band. The singer was screaming out some song about everything being broken, which pretty much summed up my life right now. Mom stared at her wineglass and ran one fingertip around and around the rim. Karma just ate, slow and methodical. No one said anything.

The food was as dry and tasteless as paper. I couldn't swallow, couldn't choke anything past the big lump sitting in my throat. Eventually, I spat the rice into a paper napkin when no one was looking. I watched my mother's face and hoped she wouldn't ever tell me about what Mark had said. As long as Mom said nothing, I could pretend I didn't know. And as long as I didn't know, I wouldn't have to make any decisions. "Someone called for you, Dylan," Karma said suddenly.

"When? I've been home all evening."

Karma shrugged. "I was in the den and I didn't feel like coming upstairs to get you."

I glared at her. "I can't believe you sometimes. Did you at least take a message?" Toni, I thought hopefully. Maybe it was Toni.

"Um, a guy." Karma screwed up her face like I was demanding some huge feat of memory. "Maybe Jack?"

"Jax."

"Yeah. Jax." Karma looked sideways at me. "Is he your boyfriend? I bet he is."

"God, Karma. What is it with you? You're obsessed with boyfriends. You're as bad as Toni." Though to be fair, Toni wasn't obsessed with having a boyfriend. She just always had one.

Mom frowned. "Dylan. Be nice."

I pushed my chair away from the table. "I'm not hungry. Can I be excused?"

"You haven't eaten anything."

"I said I'm not hungry." I gritted my teeth together, fighting back tears.

"Is this about me and Scott? Because I'm sorry if you were embarrassed, but I do live here too."

Karma looked interested. "Embarrassed about what? What happened?"

Mom tossed her long hair back over her shoulders. The green lizard peeked out from under her T-shirt, its tail curling across her collarbone. "Dylan came home when Scott and I were having a little cuddle on the couch."

"Ewwww…gross."

I shook my head. "Whatever. I don't care." I stared at my plate of rice. Little white grains, piled up like a heap of maggots. I imagined them all moving and crawling around. Someday, that'd be all that was left on the planet.

Rats and maggots, death and decay. The stench would be unbearable. I took a shallow breath and clenched my fists under the table.

Had I always been this selfish? What was wrong with me? Any decent person—any normal person—would have just said yes. No hesitation. *Yes, of course I'll help your kid. Of course I'll help Casey.* For a moment, I pictured the big-eyed kid in the photograph and life itself seemed as fragile as an eggshell and as precarious as Humpty Dumpty wobbling on his wall.

I shook my head, trying to dislodge the image. "I have to go make a phone call," I said. Without waiting for a response, I stood up, walked as fast as I could up to my room, and dialed Jax's number.

He answered right away. "Yeah?"

"It's Dylan. Did you call?"

"Yeah. Where were you?"

"Nowhere." I lay down on my bed and stuck my feet up on the wall. I could see the dirty heel-smudges I'd left behind from doing this a thousand times before. "I was home, but my sister was too lazy to come upstairs to find me."

"Yeah? Well, listen, I was wondering what you were doing later."

"Tonight?"

"No, next Wednesday." He laughed. "Duh. Yeah, tonight."

He probably thought I was an idiot. "Sorry. Um. I don't know. I mean, nothing. I'm not doing anything."

"Want to hang out? I can come by and pick you up."

I hesitated. It was Monday evening, and Mom wasn't wild about me being out late on school nights. On the other hand, if she was going to spend the afternoons smoking weed and making out with her boyfriend, she could hardly object. "Sure," I said. "I'll see you soon."

⌒

Mom looked out the window and drew in a sharp breath. "Is that your date?"

"He's not a *date*." I watched Jax approach the house.

"Well, he's good-looking all right." Mom's tone made it sound like a bad thing.

"What's your problem?" I asked.

"No problem." She leaned forward, peering into the darkness outside. "Dylan! A motorbike? You didn't tell me he was picking you up on a motorbike."

"Less fuel consumption than a car," I said, lifting my chin and flipping my hair off my face. The thought of seeing Jax buoyed me up, made me feel tougher and harder, made me not care so much about everything. "You should get rid of that station wagon, you know. It's an environmental hazard. Time to join the twenty-first century, Mom."

"Don't change the subject." Mom glanced through the kitchen door into the living room, where Karma was curled on the couch with a book, and lowered her voice. "You know that's how Sheri was killed."

"Sheri was drunk. She drove into a hydro pole. That doesn't mean motorbikes are inherently dangerous."

"Drop the sarcasm, Dylan. And the attitude. Christ. The world does not revolve around you, you know. I know you're upset…"

"Try seriously pissed off, Mom. That'd be closer."

"Is this still about the photographs?" She narrowed her eyes at me. "I don't expect you to see it this way, but I was doing you a favor."

My heart started to race. "I don't want to talk about it. I don't want to talk about Mark. I don't want to talk about you lying to me. Okay?" I stepped away from her. "I have to go."

She opened her mouth like she was going to say something; then she stopped and sighed. "Okay. Go." She caught my arm as I pushed past her, and gave me a hard look. "Jesus, baby. What's with all the face paint?"

"It's just eyeliner." My cheeks felt hot. I didn't wear makeup often because it made me look like a kid playing dress-up. I wanted to look older, not younger. I wished I had time to go and check in a mirror, but I could hear

Jax coming up the porch stairs, and I didn't want to leave him alone with my mom. "It's no big deal. Everyone wears eyeliner."

She shook her head. "Just be careful. Please?"

"I always am." I snapped my chewing gum, spat it into the garbage and walked down the stairs to the front door.

THIRTEEN

"Where are we going?" The wind tore my words away. I leaned closer to Jax, so that my helmet was almost touching his. "Where are we going?" I yelled.

Jax shouted something back, but I couldn't make it out. It didn't matter anyway, I decided. I closed my eyes and felt the wind on my face as we flew down the road. Speed. There was nothing like this feeling. It erased my anxiety, drove all thoughts out of my mind. We could crash, I told myself, but I didn't care. Everyone had to die eventually, and there were worse ways to go. *Like leukemia.*

Jax took a corner fast, and I tried to keep my body aligned with his as he leaned the bike to one side. I hoped I was doing it right. He'd made a comment before about his ex-girlfriend being a bad passenger, and while I didn't quite know what that meant, I certainly didn't want to be one. He'd turned onto the curving road that circled the university campus, and I wondered again where we were going. Finally, he pulled to a stop and turned to look at me.

"Okay?"

I grinned, trying to look casual and carefree, and lifted my helmet off, shaking my hair loose. "Good."

"My brother's in residence here. First year. Here, I'll take that. You can hop off." He took my helmet. "He's having a few friends around for drinks. I said I'd stop by. Okay?"

"Yeah, great." I'd never been in a university residence before. I could hardly wait to tell Toni. Assuming Toni was still speaking to me.

&

The room was small and neat, with a single bed along one wall, a desk and dresser on the other. Three girls and a guy were sitting on the bed; another guy was straddling a chair backward and a third was perched on the edge of the desk, holding a plastic Slurpee cup in two hands.

The guy on the bed stood up as we entered. He grinned widely. "Hey, you made it." He punched Jax's shoulder lightly. "Yo, little bro."

"Not so little," one of the girls said. She laughed.

I waited for Jax to introduce me, but he didn't. I shifted awkwardly from one foot to the other and smoothed down my hair, which was all messy from the helmet and the wind.

Jax's brother handed us each a beer. "You'll have to excuse my rude little brother. He's never had any manners. I'm Jason. Jaxon and Jason." He made a face. "Awful, huh? Our parents thought it was cute."

"I'm Dylan." I took the beer and couldn't help smiling.

"Shuffle over," Jason ordered. The three girls groaned but moved down to the pillow end of the bed. They were all pretty in a casual, confident, unconcerned-about-appearances kind of way. Everyone introduced themselves, and I instantly forgot all their names. I often had trouble with names: I always got so worried about what I was going to say that I'd forget to even listen to the introduction.

I was about to perch cautiously on the other end of the bed, but Jax sat first and pulled me down so I was sitting on his lap. I felt my cheeks growing hot, but I didn't want to draw more attention to myself by objecting. I took a swig of beer and sat awkwardly on his legs, hoping I wasn't too heavy.

"So you go to school here?" I asked Jason. Duh. Obviously. Could I make myself look like any more of an idiot?

He just smiled though. He wasn't as good-looking as Jax—heavier, with glasses, a rounder, softer face and a goatee—but he had a nice smile. "Yeah. Computer science. I was here first actually. Jax and my parents followed me."

The others were all talking and kidding around now. I knew I should join in, but I couldn't seem to do it. Twice I tried to speak, but no one heard me. Besides, I didn't really have anything to say. I didn't belong here. I felt prickly and antsy, like my skin was too tight. Jax's arm was heavy around my shoulders, and it was hard to sit still. I just wanted to get away.

"Is there a washroom around?" I asked.

One of the girls—Courtney, maybe—nodded. "Straight down the hall. Want me to show you?"

"No, I'll find it."

Out in the hallway, I drew a deep breath. I felt like I might start crying. I just couldn't seem to do this sort of thing. What the hell was wrong with me? I walked down the hall, and around the corner; then I stopped and leaned against the wall. I needed to talk to Toni. I hesitated for a moment. What if she was still furious with me? I didn't think I could cope with that right now. But I couldn't stand having this awful tension between us. I sat down on the floor and pulled out my cell.

Toni picked up right away. "Dylan?"

"Hi, yeah, it's me." I plunged forward. "Look, I'm so sorry about what I said. I mean, as soon as I said it I wished I hadn't."

"It's okay. Me too. I shouldn't have said that about you being jealous either."

I let out a long sigh. "I was such an idiot. I don't know what's wrong with me. I'm so glad you're not mad."

"I hate fighting with you," Toni said. "I mean, I really hate it."

"Yeah." We'd never really fought before, but this year, since the start of grade eleven, things had been all out of kilter. It was because of Finn, but it wasn't exactly his fault. It was like an ecosystem—introducing some new non-native plant or animal could throw everything else off balance and end up destroying a whole world. Like the rabbits in Australia: They'd been introduced as a non-native animal and they'd overrun the country within a few years, eating all the grass the sheep needed and causing all kinds of problems. I pictured Finn and frowned. There was something rather rabbity about his mouth.

"What are you up to?" Toni asked.

"You won't believe this."

"Tell me!"

"I'm at the university, at a party. With Jax." It wasn't exactly a party, but Toni didn't need to know that.

"Shut up. You, at a party?"

"Yeah. His brother's in residence here."

"Wow." Toni was quiet for a moment. When she spoke again, it was with a hint of reservation. "I thought you told me this morning that nothing was going on with you and Jax."

I nodded. It felt like a long time ago. "I know. I didn't think he was interested, but we went out together after lunch—I ended up skipping class."

"You skipped? You? No way."

"Way. I didn't exactly mean to." I hesitated, wondering how much to say. "We just went for a ride on his motorbike."

There was a pause. I could hear a second voice—a guy's voice—and Toni's muffled reply. Scratchy static. "Dylan? You still there?"

"Uh-huh."

"Finn says..." She broke off. "Just be careful, okay? With Jax?"

"What do you mean?"

"Finn says he has a bit of a rep, that's all."

"What kind of a rep?" I asked. My voice sounded stiff to my own ears, and I wasn't surprised that Toni backed down.

"Ah, you know. The usual."

I didn't say anything.

Toni spoke again. "Sorry. Are you okay?"

I almost couldn't answer. "Not very," I whispered. "Um, Toni? After school today? I went to see Mark. You know. My father."

"Really? Shit. Does your mom know?"

"Not yet."

"Wow. That's intense. So…how did it go?"

"I don't know." The lump in my throat was back. "Not so good."

"Look, let's hang out at lunch tomorrow, okay? And talk about it all then?"

"Tomorrow?"

"Is that okay? It's just, Finn is here. And you should probably get back to your party anyway, right?"

I swallowed painfully. "Don't tell Finn, okay? About Mark, I mean."

Toni sounded offended. "As if I would."

"No. I know. I'll talk to you tomorrow." I disconnected and sat there for a minute. Then I walked slowly back down the hall to find Jax and the others.

∽

Jax handed me another beer. "All right?"

I shook my head. "Fine, but I don't want another."

"You sure? I already opened it."

"Yeah. Sorry." Everyone else seemed to think that getting drunk was fun, but the couple of times I had tried it, I'd just felt sick and giddy and spent the whole of the next day worrying about whether I'd said anything stupid. Even that party at Jessica's—I'd only had a few drinks and I'd felt lousy afterward.

"No problem." He tipped the bottle up to his own lips and drank.

"So, Dylan," Jason said. "Jax was telling us you just met your dad for the first time. That's pretty wild."

There was a roaring in my ears and a feeling in my belly like the floor was dropping away beneath me. I turned to Jax. "You *told* them?"

He shrugged. "It's no big deal."

"It is to me."

"Sorry, Dyl. I didn't know." Jax put his hand on mine and pulled me down beside him on the bed.

I resisted for a moment. Everyone was staring at me. I could feel their eyes even without looking up. My face felt hot. "It's all right," I said slowly. Maybe I had over-reacted. I let myself sink down next to him. "Sorry. It's just all kind of new. I'm not used to talking about it, that's all."

Jason nodded. "That's cool." He looked at Jax. "You heard her, man. Change the subject."

"Sure." Jax ran his hand down my back, cool and casual, like we'd been going out for ages. "What's up for next weekend?"

Everyone started talking about bands and parties and clubs. I let the conversation wash over me. My thoughts were all over the place, a whirlwind of spiky fragments. Mark. Casey. Little children with big eyes and no hair. Hospital beds. Bone marrow.

I pressed my hands against my hip bones and tried to breathe normally, but anxiety flared in my chest and rushed like acid through my veins.

No one taught you this in chemistry, but fear was corrosive. It could eat you away from the inside.

Fourteen

The evening dragged on, all talk and laughter. I tried to act as if I belonged, but my mind kept slipping back to Casey and Mark.

Jax should have known I wouldn't have wanted everyone to know about Mark. That it was private. I leaned away from him and glanced at my watch. Christ. "It's ten o'clock," I told him. "I'm supposed to be home already."

He groaned and didn't move.

"Take her home, doofus. Before she turns into a pumpkin." Jason stretched out a foot and kicked his brother. "Go on."

Outside, Jax put his arm around my waist and pulled me close. Then his lips were on mine. I tried to relax and kiss him back, but my crazy brain wouldn't switch off. What if he thought I was a lousy kisser? You were supposed to open your mouth, but how much? And the whole tongue thing...it all seemed kind of weird. Did other people think about all this? I tried to stop thinking and enjoy it.

Jax's hands were low on my back, sliding down, slipping over the back pockets of my jeans. *A bit of a rep...* I wondered what exactly Finn had heard, and I pulled away, twisting my head to one side. "Hey. We should go."

"Mmm...yeah. Okay." He released me slowly and handed me a helmet. "Hop on."

I wondered a little anxiously if he was okay to drive. I wasn't sure how many beers he'd had. Just two, I thought. Three, maybe. Not that many, but I knew what my mother would say: Call a cab. Mom didn't understand though. I'd look like an idiot if I refused to get on the bike.

I looked at Jax, who was already on the bike and waiting for me, his leather jacket and helmet making him oddly anonymous. The air was damp and cold and thick with fog. I climbed on behind him and wrapped my arms tightly around his waist. "Let's go." Flying down the road, my nose and cheeks and hands turned to ice in the cold wind. Jax's leather jacket was silky against my bare forearms. I felt so incredibly alive. And yet, just like that, I could be dead. It was so strange. It just didn't seem possible that you could be here one minute and gone the next.

Finally Jax slowed down and started to pull over in front of my house. The living-room light was on, the car was in the driveway, and I could see the shadowy outline of my mother sitting on the unlit front porch. Still up. Waiting for me.

I wondered if Mark had called her. "Don't stop," I said urgently. "Keep driving."

He laughed and sped up. "Where to?"

"Anywhere."

He turned south, heading to the waterfront, and finally pulled into a parking spot along the grassy area where people walk their dogs. I didn't think I'd ever been there at night. It was very dark, and I could smell the ocean. I shivered, slipped off the bike and tucked my hands inside my sleeves.

Jax took off his helmet and looked out across the grass to where the land fell away in a steep cliff, dropping down to the rocky beach below. "It's cool, being right on the ocean."

"I'm used to it." I handed him my helmet. "It's beautiful though. I love it."

The grass was soft and spongy-wet under my sneakers as we walked toward the water. Far away, a few lights moved slowly in the darkness: ships traveling through the strait.

Above us, the sky was a dark milky gray, the stars hidden behind heavy cloud and damp fog. A long staircase led down to the beach, too narrow to walk comfortably side by side. I followed Jax down, listening to his feet thunking softly against the wooden steps and watching the way his blond-brown hair barely brushed the collar of his leather jacket. In the darkness ahead, I could hear the waves breaking on the shore.

At the base of the steps, a jumbled mess of driftwood was strewn across the ground. We clambered across it, using our hands for balance on the slippery wood. The tide was high and the beach just a narrow strip of wave-polished stones. Jax sat down on a huge water-washed log and looked at me. "Hey. Come here."

I hesitated for a moment, picked up a rock and turned its cold smooth solidness in my hand before I tossed it into the water. I wondered if he'd brought me to the beach because he liked it here and wanted to share that with me, or just because it was more private than going to a coffee shop or something. Not that I didn't want to be alone with him. It just made me nervous.

"Come here," he said again.

I pulled my jacket down to cover my butt and sat down beside him. The log felt cold and damp under my thighs. "It's wet."

"So sit on my lap." Jax grinned at me.

"I'm okay where I am."

"You're kind of shy, hey? It's cute."

I blushed. "Not really. I just, you know." I wanted to know if he thought of me as his girlfriend, or if I was just someone he was hoping to fool around with.

"Nope. I don't know."

"Um. I guess I'm just wondering about us, you know. What we're doing."

He stretched his legs out in front of him, digging two holes in the stones with the heels of his boots. "We're sitting on a beach, Dylan."

"Yeah. But…"

"I know what you mean."

I peeled off a wet strip of wood and watched it fall to the ground. "And?"

He turned to face me, lifting one leg and swinging it around so that he was straddling the log. "What do you want me to say?"

This was awful. I couldn't answer that. I just wanted to end the conversation. "I don't know. I don't want you to say anything."

"Okay then."

"Okay."

He shrugged. "So."

I felt like we'd just had a fight or something—
awkward and uncomfortable and not sure what had just
happened. "Jax…"

He stood. "Let's walk."

I walked in silence beside Jax, my feet slipping and
sinking in the loose stones. I didn't know what my
problem was. I'd just ruined what should have been a
nice moment. If I'd just sat down on his lap, I'd be back
there, kissing Jax. Instead I was walking along the beach
and wondering what he was thinking. Probably he was
wishing he'd picked some other girl to hang out with.

Jax kicked a piece of driftwood aside. "My dad, you
know, my mom's husband, he's not really my dad."

"He's not?" I wondered if telling me this was his way
of apologizing for telling Jason and his friends about
my dad.

"My mom and him split up when Jason was a baby,
and she got pregnant by this other guy she got involved
with. They got back together a couple of years later."
He didn't look at me. "Technically, Jason's my half brother."

I thought of Casey. "But you guys grew up together,
right? So that's what really makes you brothers. Like
Karma. She's not related to me at all and she only moved
in with us three years ago, but I still see her as my sister."
More than Casey anyway.

"Yeah? Your mom adopted her or something?"

"Our moms were best friends in high school. Karma's mom put my mom in her will as her kid's guardian, just in case anything happened to her. My mom did the same." I still had trouble believing this, since Sheri had been a drug addict who'd spent most of Karma's first eight years couch surfing. And my mom thought she'd be a good guardian for me? Mom said she always meant to change that part of her will, only she never got around to it. She probably still hadn't changed it.

"What happened to her parents?"

"Her mom died in a motorbike accident," I said briefly. "And her dad wasn't part of the picture. So, did you ever meet your real dad?"

"Yeah. A few times, when I was younger." He made a face. "Brent. He used to work with my mom, but he lives in New York now."

What was it with mothers and their secrets? I looked at Jax's face and wondered who he looked like, and whether he ever looked in the mirror and thought about that himself. "You don't think of him as your dad?"

"Nah. My parents got back together when I was two, and I've always thought of them as Mom and Dad. I couldn't care less about Brent."

I nodded and turned away, squinting into the opaque darkness ahead. Just ahead of us, washed by the breaking waves, something was lying on the beach. A lump of gray, a solid shape. I squinted, focused, and the image sharpened, like a camera zooming in. A seal. Sleek and inert. Dead. My chest tightened. It suddenly felt intensely important—crucial—that Jax not see it. Seeing a dead seal together would be a terrible omen. It would ruin everything, spoil every possibility.

I stopped walking and stepped behind him, so that he would turn away from the dead body. "Jax!"

He looked at me, startled.

Out of the corner of my eye, the seal's body shifted slightly, pushed by the force of the waves. I wondered why it had died and thought of the city sewage pumped out into the sea every day, the floods of bacteria and detergent and the countless toxic chemicals surging through the dark water. There were a million reasons the seal could have died.

"Come here," I said, my voice breaking. Jax turned to me, his eyebrows raised in a silent question. I stepped in close, lifted my face toward him, reached one hand up to touch his shoulder and pressed my lips against his. His mouth was so warm. I wondered if my lips felt ice cold to him. Jax touched the back of my neck, his fingers sliding under my hair.

I closed my eyes, but I could still see the seal. I could picture the milk-clouded eyes, the heavy weight of it. My stomach felt tight and my whole body ached with a deep, bone-grinding anxiety. Jax unzipped my jacket and slid his hands inside, under my sweater, across the skin of my back. I shivered, but I didn't stop him. I wasn't sure I really wanted to do this, but it was definitely easier than talking about Mark.

Jax slipped off his jacket and spread it out on the beach, pulling me down to lie beside him. One of his hands caressed my ribs and slipped under my sports bra. I couldn't believe this was happening. Toni did this kind of thing all the time. Lots of girls did. It was no big deal, I told myself. But it was to me. I felt like someone else. Some other girl.

Right now, that was better than feeling like me.

FIFTeen

Even with Jax's leather jacket lying beneath me, I could feel the beach's cold stones, knobby and hard against my spine. The fog made the world seem oddly shrunken, and I felt weirdly disconnected from what was happening. His breath was hot on my neck, one hand thrust between us, fumbling with the button of his jeans.

"Jax." I tried to work my hands between our bodies to push him away from me. "Jax!"

"Yeah." He kissed my collarbone and unzipped his jeans.

I couldn't do this. "I don't want to, I'm not…"

"Oh, come on, Dylan." He started kissing me again, his mouth muffling my words.

"No. Not here, anyway. Not like this." I felt a flash of fear—what if he wouldn't listen? I pushed him away, harder this time, and turned my face away from his mouth. "I mean it, Jax. Stop it."

"Shit." He groaned and rolled off me. "Seriously?"

"Yeah." I sat up.

He looked at me and I couldn't read his face at all. "You know, some guys would call you a tease."

"I'm not—I mean, I didn't mean to be. I just don't think, you know..."

He crouched beside me, straightening his shirt. "Come on. You're not a virgin, are you?"

"Yeah." My face burned. I wasn't about to tell him that, before tonight, I'd never done more than kiss, and not even much of that.

"No way." He sat back and looked at me. "I figured everyone had done it by grade eleven."

"Yeah, well. Guess I'm a little behind."

He grinned. "I kind of like the idea of being your first."

"What makes you so sure you will be?" I said, annoyed.

"Oh, I will." He winked and held out a hand to me. "Come on, Cinderella. I'd better get you home before midnight."

We headed back through the trees and up the long dark flight of stairs. The railing was smooth and cool under my hand, and the sound of waves on stone followed us, gradually growing distant.

I could still feel his hands all over my body.

❧

Jax drove me home in silence, and I wondered if, despite his joking around, he was angry. In front of my house, he hopped off the bike and gave me a hand down. He lifted the helmet off my head. "I was hoping you might come out again tomorrow."

"I don't think I can."

Jax reached out a hand, tried to pull me close.

"My mother might be watching," I whispered, and I pulled away.

❧

Mom was still waiting for me, sitting outside in the dark on an upside-down ceramic pot. "Come sit down with me for a minute." She patted another plant pot, gesturing for me to sit beside her. There were empty plant pots everywhere. She was always saying she was going to create this green, sun-filled space for reading and lounging, but she never did anything about it. It was just a narrow wooden porch, littered with dead leaves and cigarette butts.

I perched my butt gingerly against the railing, far enough away that Mom wouldn't smell the beer on my breath. There was an empty wineglass on the railing so probably she'd had a few drinks herself. Mom studied me for a moment. My cheeks felt warm and I was glad of the darkness. I felt like she'd be able to tell from my blush exactly what Jax and I had been doing down on the beach. I looked away from her and sniffed the air. "Are you smoking up? You know how much Karma hates it."

She shook her head defensively. "Just a little. And I hardly ever do anymore, you know that. Did I tell you, Julia just had a lump taken out of her breast? It turned out to be nothing but still…" She made a face. "Inhaling carcinogens isn't half as much fun as it used to be."

"Right. Well, please don't let Karma find you doing it, okay? It freaks her out."

"Oh relax, Dylan." She shook her head. "And give me some credit, would you? Karma's asleep."

I didn't say anything.

The people who lived in the downstairs apartment of the duplex were home for once, playing country music— a slow sad song, a husky-voiced woman singing about losing the one man she'd truly loved. I waited to see if I was going to get a lecture. For Jax, for the motorbike, for the twenty-five minutes past ten o'clock.

"Baby. You and that boy…You will be careful?"

My face was hot. "I'm not you, okay, Mom? I have no intention of repeating the family history."

Mom looked stung, but she didn't say anything. I looked at her more closely. Her eyes looked sad and sort of bruised. She'd been crying. Probably she and Scott had had a fight; that'd fit her usual pattern. I didn't care and I definitely didn't want to hear about it. "I'm going to bed," I said.

She leaned toward me. "Dylan. We need to talk."

My heart sped up. *Please don't tell me about Mark. Don't tell me, don't tell me, don't—*

"Mark called." She let out a long unsteady breath. "He said you went to see him today."

"Oh." I folded my arms across my chest. "Well, you wouldn't tell me what was going on and I thought... I wanted to know. And I wanted to see him again." The last words slipped out, catching me by surprise, and I could feel my face and neck and ears turning red.

"And he took advantage of the opportunity to manipulate you into doing what he wants. Goddamn it, Dylan. I was going to tell you."

I shrugged, not looking at her. I didn't know whether I believed her. "Yeah, well."

"So. You know then. About..."

"His daughter. Casey. Yeah, he told me." I wanted to tell her that I was going to do it. I tried to form the words, string them together, but somehow they didn't come. I didn't feel much of anything. I sat there, saying nothing.

"I wish you'd waited. I just needed some time to sort out what I was feeling."

My mother was always sorting out her feelings. Apparently it hadn't occurred to her that this wasn't really about her at all. Mark wasn't her father. It wasn't her bone marrow that Casey needed.

"You should have told me," I said.

"I was worried that you'd be hurt."

"Yeah, well. Now I know, don't I?"

"Pickle…can we talk about this?"

"It's late," I said. "I have school tomorrow."

Mom ran her fingers along the inside of her own wrist, touching the green hummingbird lightly. I hated that hummingbird now that I'd seen its twin on Mark's wrist. It was visible proof of her lies. Every time I glimpsed a flash of its green and red feathers, another wave of sick anger crashed into me.

"It's up to you, you know," she said.

But it wasn't, not really. There was no decision to make. If I didn't do it and Casey died, I'd hate myself forever. Everyone who ever knew would hate me. Fury swelled in my chest, choked the words in my throat. I looked away from her, out into the darkness. "Why should I do anything for him?" I said. "He's never even wanted to meet me and now he just shows up and wants my bone marrow? It's…" I trailed off and turned back to my mother. She was crying. Face hidden behind her hands, shoulders shaking inside her black hoodie. "Mom? What is it?"

She didn't answer right away and fear flashed through me. "Mom? What's wrong?"

She took a deep shuddering breath, wiped her eyes and looked up at me. "He never knew."

"Who? Mark, you mean? Never knew what?"

"When I got pregnant...he was already with Lisa... and I never...I just left." She reached over and put her hand on my arm. "I moved out west. I never told him."

There was a painful thud in my chest and a roaring in my ears. I flung her hand off as if it were burning me. "About me? He never knew about me?"

"I thought it would be better. Easier."

I stood up, wanting to get away from her. Hating her. "Easier for who, exactly?" I stepped toward the front door. "For you? Because it wasn't easy for me, thinking he never even wanted to meet me."

"Dylan. I'm sorry. Please listen. Let me explain." She was crying again, and it made me furious.

"I don't want to hear it," I spat the words out. "You lied. Again. How am I supposed to believe anything you say, Mom? You make me sick."

"Dylan, I wanted to tell you, lots of times. I just..."

"I don't want to talk about it," I said. "Just tell Mark I'll do it."

I watched as her fingers traced the hummingbird tattoo. "I knew you would. He was in *tears*, Dylan. On the phone."

I stared at her and slowly realized something: she was *relieved*. She had actually thought I might refuse. That was the only reason she had told me the truth. But if she could think that I'd let a little kid die just to get back at my father, she didn't know me at all. She didn't know me, and I didn't know her either. I looked away from the bright lie of the colors on her wrist, away from the tentative smile that was starting to lift the corners of her lips, and stared at the fog closing in. "I'm going to bed," I told her, and my voice seemed flat, as if it could barely travel through the milky thickness of the air.

sixteen

When I opened my eyes, Mom was standing beside my bed watching me. I groaned, rolled over and pulled a pillow over my head. "Mom. Could you not do that watching-me-sleep thing? It creeps me out."

"Sorry, Pickle."

I lay still for a moment, hoping she'd go away, thinking about what she'd told me last night. How she'd lied. I could feel her watching me even with the pillow over my head, and I hoped she was feeling guilty. Though she never seemed to feel guilt: that was my specialty.

I gave up, rolled over and rubbed my eyes. "What is it?"

"Nothing, nothing. You slept through your alarm, and I was just coming to wake you up."

"Uh-huh." I sat up and swung my legs over the edge of the bed, and last night's conversation came crashing back. "Okay. I'm up. Now can you please leave?"

She stood there for a moment, still watching me.

"*What?*"

"Nothing. See you downstairs."

I got up and pulled my housecoat from the hook on my bedroom door. I usually liked the fall, but this year I hated it. So much darkness. It wasn't even light out yet. I stared at my reflection in the mirror, turning my head this way and that. I could see flashes of Mark in the angles of my jaw, the curve of my mouth, the slight tilt of my eyes. Weird. It was all so weird.

I glanced at the clock and picked up my phone to call Toni.

"Hey."

"Dylan?"

"Yeah…can you still hang out at lunch? There's some stuff I need to talk to you about."

There was a fraction of a second's pause before Toni answered, "Sure."

Like she's doing me a favor. I bit my lip. "You don't have to."

"I just said yes. I'll hang out with you." Toni sounded annoyed.

I knew I was sounding too insecure, but I couldn't stop myself. "Only if you want to. I mean, it's okay if you'd rather be with—"

"I want to, all right?"

We used to hang out every lunch hour. It was a given. Just like talking on the phone every morning. Now I felt like I'd annoyed her somehow, and I suddenly didn't feel like talking anymore. "All right," I said. "I'll see you at school then." I hung up the phone and wondered if all friendships got messed up when people started dating. Maybe they did. Maybe the days of real friendships—the staying up late talking, giggling, planning things, counting on each other—were over. Maybe that was just something you had when you were a kid.

❧

I stared at a bowl of cornflakes swimming in soy milk. I wasn't hungry.

Karma slid her plate toward me. "Want some of my toast?"

I shook my head. "No, thanks."

"Are you okay? You look kind of…funny."

If Karma was noticing, I must really look like crap. Though maybe she was still worried because of what happened yesterday. I still hadn't told her what Mark had said or why I'd been so upset. I tried to smile a little. "I'm fine."

Mom put down her newspaper and looked at me with raised eyebrows.

I didn't want to get into a conversation about it—actually, I didn't want to talk to my mother at all, ever—but I needed to know what was going to happen next. "So, do I have to get a blood test or something?" I asked.

Karma's eyes widened, and she opened her mouth to speak.

"That's the first step." Mom poured enough milk into her coffee to turn it almost white. "I just called Mark and told him that you'd do it."

"You did? Was he…was he pleased?" I hated myself for asking.

Karma was practically wriggling off her chair in frustration. "What are you talking about? Pleased about what?"

Mom's eyebrows drew together in a frown. "Of course he was pleased. What else would he be?"

I shrugged. I didn't know why I'd asked that or what I'd meant, exactly.

"Anyway. He's staying longer than he'd planned. His wife and daughter are flying out on Thursday. Apparently they're going to take Casey to some naturopath in Vancouver." She drank her coffee, not looking at me.

"Mark says he's probably a quack, but I guess they're feeling they have to try everything, you know?"

"But if I'm a match, that'll help, right? She could be all right."

"What's wrong with her?" Karma sounded like she was about to explode.

Mom held up one hand to tell Karma to wait. "Pickle…I don't really know the first thing about it. I guess that's the hope, but I don't think there are any guarantees."

There never were. I closed my eyes for a moment and stared at the prickles of light in the darkness. Like tiny stars. Reluctantly, I opened them again and looked at Karma. "Mark's kid has leukemia, and he wants me to get tested to see if I can be a bone marrow donor."

"Ohhh." Her round face was serious. "So that was why he wanted to see you."

I realized that I had no idea how he had found out I existed. "Yup. Exactly. That was the reason." My voice was louder and higher pitched than usual.

There was a heavy pause. Mom ran one finger along the table edge. "He thought you might like to meet her. Casey."

"Me? Why would I want to?"

"Maybe he thinks you'll want to help more if you meet her. I don't know."

"I already *said* I'd do it."

"I know. Don't bite my head off."

Karma looked thoughtful. "Maybe he thought you'd want to meet her because you're, you know, sort of related."

I looked across the table at her. It was strange: we'd only been living together for three years and we weren't even blood relatives, but I loved her, even though she drove me crazy. Somehow we had become a family. We had become sisters.

But I didn't think of Casey as a sister at all.

⁂

The first time I met Karma, she was eight and I was thirteen. Mom flew to Toronto to pick her up, and I stayed behind with her friend Julia for a few days while all the legal stuff got sorted out. I'd known for a few weeks that she was coming—we'd rearranged furniture, turned Mom's tiny office into a third bedroom—but I couldn't get my head around the idea that she wouldn't just be visiting. It had been just me and Mom for my whole life, and it didn't seem possible that a third person could suddenly join our family.

And finally they'd arrived. Julia and I drove to the airport to meet them. Mom, looking exhausted, was carrying an unfamiliar leather suitcase and pulling her own wheeled one, and this skinny kid was tagging along behind, clutching a small ratty-looking backpack.

"Karma, this is my daughter Dylan," Mom said.

I thought it was strange that she said it that way around—like the introduction was for Karma, not me. I tried to push away a surge of jealousy and forced a smile. "Hi, Karma. Nice to meet you."

She just stared at me with big dark-lashed eyes. She was wearing embroidered jeans that were too short for her and a black T-shirt with *Long Live Rock 'n' Roll* written on it in silvery letters. The shirt had ridden up so I could see a strip of her tummy: brown skin and an outie belly button. She stuck her fingers in her mouth and sucked on them.

I turned to my mom. "Want me to take one of those cases?"

She handed me the leather suitcase, which I figured was Karma's, and leaned close to me. "Speaking of cases," she whispered into my ear, "Sheri's kid is a bit of a case herself. I think we're going to have our hands full."

And just like that, I felt better again. Me and my mom would always be a team. Looking after Karma was going to be something we did together, and that meant that no matter what she was like, no matter how awful it was, it would somehow be okay.

And the first weeks and months *were* awful. Karma had wicked tantrums, screaming like a toddler when she didn't get her way. Hair washing, tooth brushing, mealtimes— anything could trigger a meltdown. My mom would throw her arms up in the air and yell at her, make threats, offer bribes, and finally give up in frustration. Oddly enough, Karma was more cooperative with me, so after a while, Mom handed off some of her care to me. *Dylan, can you get Karma to eat breakfast before school? Can you make sure Karma has a bath? Can you ask Karma if she'd eat pizza for dinner?* Karma usually did what I said with no fuss at all. It annoyed my mother, but I found it rather satisfying.

I wasn't sure when things changed. It wasn't dramatic. One day I realized that Karma hadn't had a meltdown for a long time. She did okay at school, rode her bike everywhere, and started playing baseball. Sometimes I wondered how much she thought about her mom and how she felt about this new life, but they weren't questions I felt I could ask.

Karma was one of the most private people I'd ever met.

Mom had told me a bit about Sheri: that she'd had a rough childhood, that she'd had a bit of a problem with drugs, that some of her boyfriends hadn't treated her well. So I had a pretty good idea how it might have been for Karma before she came to live with us. Not the details, of course—but there were some things you could guess without needing to hear them said aloud, and I didn't blame Karma for not wanting to talk about that stuff.

Karma had even less information about her dad than I had about mine. Sheri had always told her she didn't know who her father was. Karma knew she looked like him though. Sheri had been white, blond-haired and sharp-featured, but Karma had black hair, dark eyes, brown skin and a round face. Everyone always assumed she was First Nations, but Karma said she didn't even know that for sure.

There was one thing I hoped Karma did know for sure: she was my sister, and Casey could never change that.

⁓

At lunch, Toni was waiting at my locker, looking cute as ever in skinny jeans, furry boots and a pink heart-patterned hoodie. "Hey," she said, grinning widely. "I feel like I haven't seen you for ages."

I tried to grin back, but my smile felt stiff and forced. It was hard to forget the feeling I'd had on the phone the night before. I was pretty sure that Toni would rather be with Finn.

"Come on." Toni tilted her head to one side. "Cheer up."

Maybe it was just me. Maybe I was being insecure and oversensitive. Mom always said I blew things out of proportion. "Let's go somewhere we can talk. Like, outside."

It was raining—a slow, cold drizzle leaking from a lead-heavy gray sky. Toni wrinkled her nose in disgust, and I zipped up my windbreaker.

The nearby coffee shop was packed, its windows steamed up and every seat taken. Toni ordered two hot chocolates, and while she paid, I swooped down like a vulture on an about-to-be vacant table.

"Okay," Toni said as she put the drinks down. "So tell me. How's it going with Jax?"

Disposable cups. "You should have said the drinks were for here."

She rolled her eyes. "Come on. What's up?"

"I don't know if I really want a boyfriend, you know?"

"He's pretty cute. I mean, I get that." She stirred her hot chocolate, but her eyebrows were drawn together in a frown.

"What is it?"

"Don't be mad, okay?"

"Why? Is this about what Finn said about Jax?"

She nodded, still looking down at her drink. "He said he wouldn't leave his sister alone in a room with him."

"So? His sister's what, twelve?"

"Thirteen." Toni shrugged. "I don't know, Dylan. Just be careful, that's all I'm saying."

"He was kind of a jerk last night anyway. I don't know. It's not, like, the biggest thing in my life at the moment."

"Your dad?"

"Uh-huh. All that."

"You said things didn't go so well."

I stirred my drink slowly, tracing three perfect circles, and licked the spoon. "That's an understatement," I said at last. "Turns out his kid has leukemia and he wants me to be a bone marrow donor."

"Whoa." Toni leaned back. "Are you serious?"

"Yeah. Kind of weird, huh?"

"He shows up after sixteen years because he wants your blood for his kid? Jesus. That's intense."

"Bone marrow. Not blood."

"Whatever."

I scowled. "Easy for you to say. It's not your hip bone that's going to get needles stuck in it."

Toni winced. "You are going to do it though? Right?"

"Yeah. I mean, what choice do I have?"

"No choice, really." Toni took a cautious sip. "It sucks though. I figured he wanted to get to know you or something."

I watched the steam rising from my drink. "Mom told me something last night. You know how I always thought Mark never wanted to meet me?"

She nodded.

"Turns out he never even knew about me."

"What do you mean?"

The room felt too small and noisy and crowded, and sitting still suddenly seemed like torture. "Mom never told him she was pregnant."

"Whoa. You're serious?".

I nodded. There was a big lump in my throat. "Can we walk?"

Toni nodded and picked up our drinks. "See? Good thing I got to-go cups."

I followed her out the door and into the cold drizzling rain. She handed me my cup, and we started to walk. "Thanks," I said. "Too many people in there."

"So, did your mom say why?"

"Why she never told him? Or why she lied to me about it?" I shook my head. "No to both. She just said that when she realized she was pregnant, he was already with someone else—the woman he's married to now—and so she never bothered to tell him."

"Weird. I mean, I can see if she'd decided to have an abortion, but to have the baby and not tell him?" She frowned. "So how did he find out about you?"

"I don't know." I wasn't going to ask Mom either. I didn't trust anything she told me. "I'll ask Mark," I said.

"Do you have plans to see him again?"

"Not exactly." I looked at her. "What are you doing tonight?"

Toni stopped walking, turned to me and grinned. "You kidding? I'm coming with you."

seventeen

At dinner, Mom told me I'd have to miss homeroom the next day. I had an appointment in the morning for a blood test, to find out whether I might be able to be a donor for Casey.

I needed to talk to Toni and figure out how we were going to find Mark tonight. I was too restless to sit or read or do homework. I'd tried calling her, but her phone went straight to voice mail. No doubt she was talking to Finn. I stared at the phone for a few minutes, wondering what to do.

Scott and my mother were downstairs, and I didn't want to be around them. And there was nowhere else to go. I wanted to throw something—hurl something heavy right out the window. And scream. I felt as if my insides were boiling: a bubbling seething poisonous mess.

I dug my nails into the palms of my hands as hard as I could and dropped down onto my bed. *Don't freak out,* I told myself. *Get a grip.* I lay on my back and studied the dead flies in my ceiling light. Five of them. Ugh.

There was a knock at my door. "What?"

The door opened a crack, and Karma poked her face in. "Can I come in?"

I sat up, both annoyed and relieved at the distraction. "Yeah."

She inched inside the door and stood there, shifting her weight from one foot to the other.

"What's wrong?" I crossed my legs and leaned toward her. "Are you okay?"

She shrugged. "I was just wondering. You know what you said this morning? About helping Mark's kid?"

"Uh-huh. What about it?"

"I don't know. Just, you know, I realized something. You have a real sister now."

"She's not really my sister," I said quickly, "and Mark's not really my father. He's just some guy who happens to share some of the same DNA as me. That's all."

She didn't say anything.

I pulled a face. "It's like, what if you found out that your mom had had another kid and given it up for adoption or something? Or that your dad had other kids? They wouldn't really be your family."

"My dad might have," Karma said. "If I had brothers or sisters, I think I'd want to know."

"Would you?"

"Yeah. Definitely I would. They'd be family, wouldn't they? *Real* family."

"We're real family." I knew what she meant though.

"Yeah, I know. Still, I think you're lucky to meet your father. Even though, you know…"

"Even though he just wants my bone marrow."

"Yeah."

I didn't say anything for a minute. Karma had never met her dad; she didn't even know who he was. Until recently, it had been something we'd had in common.

"So are you going to meet her?" Karma asked. "If you do, can I come too?"

"No and no."

"Aren't you even curious?"

Karma, of course, was curious about absolutely everything—including things that were none of her business. I ignored the question. "I suppose Scott's still downstairs."

"Yeah. How come you don't like him?"

"How come you do?"

"He's nice. He asks questions about school and friends and my bike, all kinds of stuff. And he actually listens."

"Yeah, because he's taken all those social-worker classes on listening skills."

"It's not fake listening," Karma said.

"Sure it is."

"It's not." Karma's voice was hard-edged. "I've talked to lots of social workers, believe me."

I was silent for a moment. We never talked much about Karma's life before she came to live with us. When she first came, I was so freaked out by the idea that her mom had died that I could hardly speak to her at all. I couldn't possibly talk about her mom, and talking about anything else had felt kind of inappropriately trivial. Insensitive. Now too much time had passed and it seemed strange to bring it up. Plus, I was superstitious about discussing death. My mom's mother had died in a car accident when my mom was my age. Just the thought made me anxious. "Okay," I said at last. "So Scott's really listening. I don't talk to him, so how would I know?"

"I think Amanda's going to break up with him," Karma said. "I wish she wouldn't though."

"He's not her type."

"He is too." She looked as if she might cry.

My cell phone rang and I pounced on it. "Hello?"

"Hey. It's me."

"Toni?" I made a face at Karma and gestured toward the door. Karma hesitated for a moment, no doubt hoping to hear something interesting. Finally she left, banging the door closed behind her.

"Sorry, I've been on the phone. My aunt called."

Not Finn then. "So can you get your mom's car?"

"Yup. Is your mom going to let you go?"

"I haven't actually asked."

She laughed. "Okay. Sure. See you soon."

❦

Mom and Scott were sitting in the living room, talking in low, intense voices. Maybe Karma was right. The tone of the conversation did have that breaking-up feel to it. I'd seen it plenty of times before.

"Mom?"

She looked irritated. "What is it?"

"I'm going out with Toni, okay? Just for a bit."

"Dylan, it's…" She broke off to look at her watch. "It's almost nine. A bit late to be going out."

A hard ball of anger was lodging itself in my chest, right in the hollow between my collarbones. "I need to talk to someone, Mom. And apparently you're busy."

She stood up. "Don't be like that. If you want to talk to me, you know that all you have to do is say so."

I shrugged. For no good reason, I was suddenly fighting tears. "Whatever."

"Amanda." Scott hesitated. "If you want me to leave…"

She shook her head. "I don't want you to leave."

I jumped in. "So can I go or what?"

Mom hesitated. "Yes. Okay. But don't be late. Tomorrow—"

I cut her off. "Don't worry. I'm hardly going to forget about tomorrow."

❧

Toni picked me up in her mom's Honda. Because she had a December birthday, her parents had started her in kindergarten a year late so she wouldn't always be the youngest. So she'd always been the oldest in our grade instead. This year, she'd been the first to get her driver's license, which had given her a lot of popularity points. I had decided never to get a license, on principle, but there were times—like now, when it was dark and cold and pouring rain—that cycling wasn't all that appealing.

The car was warm, heat blasting. Some electronic-sounding music I didn't recognize was playing on the car stereo, and Toni turned down the volume as I got in. "Do you know for sure that he's still at the hotel?" she asked.

"He has to be," I said. "His wife and Casey are flying out on Thursday."

She raised one eyebrow. "Seriously? Are you going to meet her?"

I shook my head. "I just want some answers, that's all. I don't want a whole new family."

"What does Karma think about it all? You having another sister, I mean?"

"I don't know. She says she'd be curious, if it was her."

Toni nodded. "Me too."

Why did everyone seem to think I should meet her? "Well, not me," I said shortly. After a couple of minutes, Toni turned the volume back up. I leaned my head against the window and watched streetlights flash past as we drove through downtown. Down by the harbor, the buildings were all lit up, fairy-tale pretty against the dark sky. "She might not make it," I said. "Casey, I mean. She's pretty sick."

Toni didn't say anything right away. She took a couple of turns, pulled into a parking spot at the side of the street across from the hotel, turned off the engine and shifted in her seat to face me. "Is that why you don't want to meet her?"

My throat ached with holding back tears. "Maybe. I don't know."

She held my gaze for a long moment. "Remember when we used to say we were going to live forever? That by the time we were old, science would have found a cure for death?"

I gave a startled laugh. "Of course. I really believed it too."

"I know you did."

"Didn't you?"

She shook her head. "I don't think so. Not really."

"I guess it was easier to believe than the alternative. Death is so *weird*." I wondered if she had ever believed that we'd live together and rescue stray dogs, or if she'd just been pretending about that too.

"Yeah. Well, we were just kids. We didn't know anything." Toni unbuckled her seat belt. "Come on. Let's go get you some answers."

❦

The front desk clerk called up to Mark's room and told us he'd be right down.

"You want me to stay?" Toni whispered.

I nodded. "Yeah. If you don't mind."

"Are you kidding? I'm dying of curiosity." She watched the elevator doors. "I can't believe I'm actually going to meet your father. Does he look like you?"

"Kind of. I don't know. Well, you'll see." I wiped my hands on my jeans and wondered where to start. Did I owe him an apology? I'd been kind of a bitch last time

I saw him, all snarky about him making small talk and then taking off when he told me about Casey.

"This is so intense," Toni said. "I'm actually kind of nervous."

I snorted. "Please. *You're* nervous?"

The elevator door opened and Mark stepped out. He was more casually dressed this time, wearing jeans and a blue sweater. Toni leaned close to me. "Dylan! He's totally hot."

"Shut up. He's totally old."

Mark waved and headed our way. I waved back.

"Hello, Dylan." He glanced at Toni. "I'm Mark Wheatcroft."

"Sorry. Toni, Mark. Mark, this is my best friend Toni. Uh…" I looked at Toni frantically and she came to my rescue as always.

"Dylan had some questions and she wanted to talk to you, so…" She shrugged. "So here we are."

"Here you are." Mark nodded solemnly, but one corner of his mouth twitched slightly, as if he was holding back a laugh. "How about we go into the restaurant and I buy you both a Coke or something?"

"I have money," I blurted out. "I mean, you don't have to pay for us."

Toni elbowed me. "Thanks. That'd be great. I'd love some tea, actually."

We took a corner table, and Mark ordered tea for all of us. "So," he said, once the waiter had gone, "I'm glad to get the chance to thank you, Dylan. For trying to help Casey. For agreeing to be tested."

"Sure. I mean, of course I would."

He smiled and I noticed that his mouth went up more on the left than the right, same as mine. "I didn't know what to expect, to be honest. I thought you might be pretty angry with me. You know, for not having been around all those years and then showing up like this."

Toni kicked me under the table.

"Yeah. Well, I kind of was." I cleared my throat. "Mom always told me you didn't want to meet me."

"But now? Did she tell you...?"

"Yeah. You never even knew about me. She never told you she was pregnant."

Mark put his hands on the table and leaned toward me. "God, I'm so glad. I can't tell you what a relief it is that you know that. I so wanted to tell you. I hated to think that you imagined I was some..."

"Deadbeat," Toni put in helpfully.

He nodded. "Mmm. Yes. Thank you."

"Why didn't you just tell me yourself?" I already knew the answer, but I wanted to hear him say it.

"When I called your mother, she agreed to let me meet you as long as I promised I wouldn't talk about any of that. And—well, I didn't want to cause problems for you or her."

"Weren't you angry though?" I asked. "I mean, that she'd never told you? Don't you think you had a right to know that you were, you know…"

"A father?" He nodded. "Yes. Very angry, at first. But I've had a couple of years to come to terms with that."

I stared at him. "What?"

"I said, I was angry, but I'd—"

Toni broke in. "Hold on. You've known about Dylan for two years?"

He looked at me, frowning. "I thought you said your mother told you."

"Not everything, I guess."

"Argh." Mark rubbed his forehead, pushing the skin into wrinkles. "I'm not sure what to do here. I don't want to create difficulties for you and Mandy. Amanda."

"She's the one who's created difficulties," I said. "I think I have a right to know the truth."

"I agree, Dylan. You do. But keep in mind, your mother was only sixteen when she found out she was pregnant. Her mom had died not that long before, and she was pretty wrecked over that. Well, you can imagine." Mark rubbed the lines on his forehead. "Her dad was no help. He cared more about getting drunk than he did about anything else. I don't know if Mandy even told him she was pregnant. They'd barely spoken since she moved out."

"She moved out? Left home, you mean? When was that?" I'd known her dad drank, and that they hadn't spoken in years, but it was driving me crazy that Mark seemed to know more of the story than I did.

He shook his head. "Look, I don't want to get in the middle of things between you and your mother. You should talk to her about this. Let her explain how it was."

"But she won't. She doesn't like talking about it." My eyes stung with tears of anger. "I don't understand why she never told you about me."

"Nor do I, not really. Maybe there isn't a logical reason, Dylan. When I got in touch with Amanda—the first time, two years ago, I mean—she tried to explain. She said she just panicked and took off. Running away from all kinds of stuff, not just me." He shook his head. "Sixteen. Same age as you. God, it's crazy, really. The whole thing. I feel pretty sick when I think about it."

The waiter arrived with pots of tea and milk and sugar, and we all took a minute to pour and stir. Toni leaned forward. "So how did you find out about Dylan?"

Mark sipped his tea and winced. "Hot." He rubbed his chin, which was faintly blue with stubble, and looked at me. "A couple of years ago, Lisa ran into an old friend— a guy called Paul, someone who had known Amanda and me and Sheri back when we were teenagers. He was a bit of a troubled guy back in those days—still is, probably. Anyway, he'd stayed in touch with Sheri and he told Lisa about Sheri's accident. He'd been to the funeral the year before, was all choked up talking about it."

I nodded. "Okay. But…"

"He told her that Sheri had a kid, a little girl, and that the kid had gone out west to live with Amanda and her daughter, who was about fourteen." Mark shook his head. "Lisa told me and I did the math. I didn't know for sure, of course, but I figured you could be… you might be…"

"This was two years ago?"

"Uh-huh. I looked online—Amanda Jarvis—and found her business, Urban Cleaners."

"Urban Organics," I corrected.

"Yeah. And I called her and asked about you."

"Two years ago." Right after Karma came to live with us. And Mom had said nothing to me. Not a word. "What did she say?"

He sipped his tea again, and when he put it back on the saucer, it clattered, and I noticed his hand was shaking slightly. "She said that yes, I was your father—though she didn't use that word. I think she said that yes, I got her pregnant, as if it was entirely my fault. She said her dad had given her some money to get rid of her—some life insurance policy from her mom's death, I think—and she'd gone out west to get a fresh start. She said she wanted me to stay away." He looked at me steadily. "And I agreed. Did I do the wrong thing, Dylan? Maybe I should have pushed harder, but I didn't want to interfere in your lives after all that time."

"Until Casey got sick."

I could see his Adam's apple jump as he swallowed. "I'm sorry." He looked at Toni for a moment and then back to me. "And I know I'm beyond preoccupied with her at the moment. Her illness has pretty much taken over our lives. But I'm glad you know that it wasn't my fault that I wasn't around. That I wasn't just an asshole, or, as your friend put it, a deadbeat."

I nodded. "I'm glad too."

"And…" He cleared his throat. "At some point, when things are more…when my life is a bit less…when Casey is better…" His voice cracked. "I really would like to get to know you, Dylan, if it isn't too late for that."

My eyes were stinging. I stared down at my tea. "Maybe," I said. "Yeah, maybe." Under the table, I felt Toni's hand squeeze my knee. "I think I better go," I said. I didn't want to start crying in front of him, and if I stayed here any longer, it'd happen for sure.

Toni scribbled something on a piece of paper and handed it to Mark. "Dylan's cell," she said. "You should call her."

I stood up. "Do me a favor?"

He nodded.

"Don't call Mom and tell her I was here."

"Fair enough." He stood, and for a second I thought he might try to hug me, but then he took a step away and held out his hand. I shook it, not meeting his eyes. He had long fingers, like me, the little one slightly crooked. As Toni and I walked across the restaurant, I could feel his eyes on our backs, watching us leave.

eighteen

Mom was in bed when I got home. I tiptoed past her room, freezing mid-stride as her light flicked on. Crap.

"Dylan?"

"Yeah?"

"Is everything okay?"

"Fine. I'm going to bed."

"Come in here for a minute."

Reluctantly, I slipped through her half-open door. "What is it?"

She patted her bed. "Just wanted to talk to you."

I stepped closer but didn't sit down.

Mom was sitting up in bed, the covers pulled up to her waist. She was bare shouldered, wearing a faded green tank top, and her bird and lizard tattoos were splashes of bright color against the white sheets. "Dylan, what's wrong? Can't we talk about it?"

"Nothing to talk about." It sounded sharper and ruder than I'd meant it to.

"Are you nervous about your appointment? It's just a quick blood test."

Thanks for reminding me. "Not really. Just, you know."

"You don't have to do anything you don't want to do. I mean, no one is going to pressure you into…"

I snorted. "Right. Casey might die, but hey, no pressure."

"Dylan." She patted the bed again. "Come sit down."

I perched on the edge of the bed.

"I know Mark showing up like this has been difficult—"

I interrupted her. "Actually, finding out that you've been lying to me my whole life has been difficult."

After a long pause, she said, "I want you to do what is right for you."

"As long as it means helping Casey?"

Mom reached out and touched my hair, brushing it away from my face. I didn't say anything. My throat was aching, and if I tried to talk, I was going to start bawling like a little kid.

"It'll all be okay," she said. "I promise."

"You can't promise that." I pulled away. "You can't just make everything be okay. It doesn't work like that."

She sighed and didn't answer for a minute. When she finally spoke, her voice sounded funny. "I know. I just wish it did."

There was an empty wineglass on her bedside table. Drinking again. I looked at her more closely. Her eyes were puffy and pink-rimmed and her nose was shiny. "Mom? Have you been crying?"

"Scott and I sort of broke up. I'm taking a break from seeing him."

"Oh." I hadn't ever wanted her to be with him, so why did I have this heart-sinking achy feeling? "Are you... I mean, was that what you wanted?"

This time she took even longer to answer. "I don't think I really know what I want."

I felt the ground shift beneath me. A flicker of sympathy—after all, I didn't know what I wanted either—and then a flood of anger. Why couldn't she just get it together and be reliable for once? With everything else that was going on, shouldn't I at least be able to count on my mother to be sane and solid and predictable?

"You're almost ," I said. The words were stiff and bitter in my mouth. "Isn't it about time you figured that out?"

She flinched. "Dylan."

I didn't wait to hear what she was going to say. I could hear her saying my name a second time, but I just walked down the hall and went to bed.

❧

The next morning, Mom was all fake-cheerful, as if she had made a decision to put last night's conversation behind her. *Tomorrow is a new day,* she always said. I thought it was the stupidest saying ever. Everything that had happened in the past just followed you into the future. One day followed another, and there was nothing really new about any of them.

"Have some breakfast." Mom was still wearing her green tank top and boxer shorts, and her hair was all messed up from being slept on.

"I'm not really hungry."

Her pseudo-smile started to slip. "Fine. I'll have to drop you off at school right after the appointment though. I'm meeting Julia."

"Fine."

"Karma, Dylan and I need to leave before you this morning, so make sure you lock up. Okay?"

Karma didn't answer, and I turned to look at her. Her eyes were red-rimmed, and she was poking at her cereal with the tip of her spoon.

"What's the matter with you?" I asked.

She shrugged and kept poking.

"Karma is a little upset that Scott and I…that we're not together right now." Mom's voice was tight.

Karma stood up. She looked at Mom, and without a word she dropped her spoon into her bowl. Milk splashed all over the table and dripped onto the floor.

"Karma!" Mom stood up too and raised her voice. "What the hell is wrong with you? You think I need this right now?"

Karma slammed out of the room.

"Well." Mom stood there uncertainly for a moment before slowly lowering herself back into her seat. "Goddamn it." She glared at me. "You're awfully quiet this morning. I hope you aren't going to be difficult too, because I don't have the energy for that right now."

"I'm always quiet in the morning." I sat down at the table and dragged a finger through Karma's milk puddles, tracing a pattern of lines on the smooth surface. Poor kid. She just wanted things to stay the same, and they never did. For a moment I wondered if I should go and talk to her, but Karma was like me—she'd rather be left alone when she was upset. Anyway, there was nothing I could say that would help.

Mom sighed. "Are you worried about the appointment?"

I wiped my milky finger on my jeans. "No. What happens next, after this?"

"They'll run tests on the blood to see if you could be a potential donor for Casey. The results will go to

Casey's doctor back in Ontario, and he'll let Mark and Lisa know."

So they'd know before I would. "And they'll call us?"

"That's right. In a couple of weeks." She hesitated. "Dylan…Don't get your hopes up about being able to help."

"What do you mean?"

"It isn't likely you'll be a match. When I spoke with Casey's doctor in Ontario about getting you tested, she said that even a full sibling has less than a thirty-percent chance of being a match. They don't usually even test half siblings."

"They don't? So why…?"

She lifted one bare shoulder and let it drop again. "Because Mark was desperate. Casey doesn't have any full siblings, which would be her best chance of a donor, and so far none of the people on the bone marrow donor registry has been a good match for her."

"But they wouldn't test me if there was no chance I'd be a match."

Mom eyed me closely. "Just don't get your heart set on this. Apparently Casey's doctor isn't hopeful."

That felt all wrong. "Isn't it her job to be hopeful? She can't just give up on Casey."

"It's her job to be realistic."

I swallowed. It sounded like I was in the same no-hope category as Casey's quack doctor in Vancouver. "So it's… a long shot."

"Yes. A very long shot." She reached across the table and put her hand on mine. Her elbow was sitting right in the middle of all that spilt milk.

I didn't say anything.

"You are helping, you know. Whatever happens." Mom's eyes were suddenly full of tears. "If Casey doesn't make it, Mark has to know he's done everything he could possibly do."

I pulled my hand away. It made me furious, her acting as if she was concerned for Mark's feelings after what she had done to him.

She stood up, turned away from me, dried her hands on a dish towel without bothering to wash them first. "Get your coat on. We have to go."

nineteen

The appointment wasn't even at a doctor's office—just a hospital lab. We sat in the waiting room for a while: plastic chairs lining the walls, people sitting around avoiding eye contact by reading magazines or staring at their hands folded in their laps. Mostly older people, although one young woman was there with a baby sleeping on her lap. Mom read a magazine, and I pretended to do the same.

Finally someone called my name and I stood up. Mom looked at me, and I shook my head to tell her I didn't need her to come with me. I followed a slim, long-haired woman into a small room and sat down in the single chair.

"Any trouble with needles?" she asked.

I shook my head. "No. I passed out once after giving blood at school, but I think it was just because I just hadn't eaten that day." Come to think of it, I hadn't eaten today either. I decided not to mention that.

She took my hand, palm up, stretched my arm out and tapped two fingers against the inside of my elbow. "Nice veins."

I looked down at the tracing of fine blue lines under my skin. "Uh, thanks, I guess."

"Just a quick pinch." The needle slid into my vein, and my blood, surprisingly dark, streamed into the vial. Her hand was steady and competent, matter-of-fact, and there were a scattering of tiny brown moles on her forearm. I wondered what her name was. Maybe she'd told me and I hadn't been listening.

"There. All done. That wasn't so bad, was it?" She stuck a cotton ball to my arm with a piece of tape.

I shook my head. "No." I stood up. Nothing tilted or slid away like it had that time at school, and I guessed I wasn't going to pass out. I felt slightly disappointed. Not that I exactly wanted to pass out—it'd be embarrassing, and Mom would freak out—but it felt odd to just go to school after this. It felt odd that I had to go on like everything was normal while we waited to find out if my bone marrow was any good.

Mom drove me to school, chattering nonstop the whole way. I shifted in my seat and loosened the seat belt where it was tugging across my shoulder.

"This weekend, hon? You remember? Me and Julia are going to that concert in Seattle?"

"Is that this weekend?"

She nodded. "We thought we'd catch a ferry Friday evening, go clubbing in Vancouver, and drive down to Seattle for the concert on Saturday. I need you to keep an eye on Karma."

"So you'll be gone for two nights? You'll be home Sunday?"

"Yeah. Sorry, Pickle. I feel kind of bad leaving right now, with everything that's going on. It's just that this concert is going to be so awesome. And we've had this planned for ages. They're Julia's absolute all-time-favorite band, you know?"

Through the layers of my jacket and sweatshirt I could feel the cotton-ball bump at the crook of my elbow. "Yeah. Well, we won't have heard anything by then anyway."

"No." Mom turned into the school parking lot and glanced at me. "You sure you don't want to meet Casey while they're here?"

I wanted to see Mark again, but I wanted it to be his idea. I wasn't going to be the one to ask. And as for Casey..."I'm sure."

Mom sat there for a moment, just looking at me.

"I gotta go." I opened my door, nodded goodbye to Mom and walked quickly into the school, breathing in the cold damp air.

Toni was standing by her locker. She had hung a small mirror on the inside of her locker door and she was looking at her reflection, pulling on her bangs and frowning.

"Hey, Toni. Your hair looks fine."

She made a face. "I wish it was straight like yours. Look at this." She pointed. "It keeps curling up. *Flipping* up. It looks stupid."

"It looks fine. Really." I wished all I had to worry about was my hair. "Want to hang out at lunch?"

"Um, maybe. I'm not sure what Finn is doing."

Finn, Toni and I all had third-period lunch. Jax had fourth. I didn't know if he'd want to spend lunch hours with me anyway, but I was glad it was a non-issue. "Well, let me know," I said, trying to keep my voice light.

"Got any plans for the weekend?"

I shook my head. "Mom's going to Seattle, so I guess I can do what I want."

Toni's eyes widened. "Have a party."

"Not a chance. Karma would tell Mom. Anyway, the downstairs neighbors complain if we make too much noise."

"So just have a few people over. Like me." She grinned.

❧

It turned out that Finn had a lunch-hour meeting for some project, so Toni was free to hang out. Part of me wanted to tell her that I'd made other plans, but I swallowed my resentment. I wanted to talk to her, and besides, she probably wouldn't believe me.

The morning clouds had cleared, and the dampness had blown from the air. A blue-sky day, as cold and clear and sharp as glass. We walked down the sidewalk. Toni kicked at a carefully raked pile of leaves on the edge of the road, scattering them wildly, and I tried not to worry that someone would see and yell at us for messing up all their work.

"Toni? Can I ask you something personal?"

"Sure."

I looked down at the sidewalk and slowed my steps. I couldn't think what words to use. Toni waited patiently, matching her steps to mine. Finally I just blurted it out.

"Do you think it's weird that I don't know if I really want to go out with Jax?"

She looked startled. "Course not."

"It's…I feel like he expects me to, you know, have sex with him. Like if I go out with him, it'll just happen, sooner or later."

"Do you want to?"

I didn't know how to answer that. "Not really. I don't know."

Toni wrinkled her nose. "If you're not sure, don't."

"But what if he thinks I should? I mean, I can't just keep saying no."

"Sure you can. If he cares about you, he'll understand. And if not, you're better off without him."

I didn't know if Jax cared about me. I didn't really feel like I knew him all that well. "Do you think if a guy tells you something about himself, like something personal, that means he likes you?"

She tilted her head and looked at me quizzically. "Whether he likes you isn't really the point. I mean, you shouldn't do anything you don't want to do. Is he, you know, pressuring you?"

"I don't know," I said again. I thought about lying on the beach with Jax. My cheeks were hot, but I asked anyway. "When you, you know, with Finn…um, do you really like it?"

"Sex, you mean? Of course. Who doesn't?" She laughed.

I felt like a little kid, like there was some knowledge that everyone had except me. Just talking to people, knowing when to look at them and when to look away, figuring out when to joke and when to be serious... it was all complicated enough without bringing sex into the equation. I couldn't imagine ever being comfortable enough to do that with another person. But Toni seemed so casual about all this stuff. I looked at her and wished I knew what to ask. It sounded like she'd gone all the way with Finn, and I wondered when that had happened. I couldn't help feeling hurt that she hadn't told me.

"So, about this weekend," Toni said. "Can I at least come over? And Finn? And maybe Jessica and Ian?"

I wondered whether to invite Jax. If I didn't, I'd be the only one who wasn't half of a couple. "I guess so. We could get some movies."

"Cool."

We were silent for two or three steps. I flexed my elbow and felt the cotton ball still there, taped to the inside of my arm. "I had that blood test this morning. You know, to see if I can help Casey."

"And?"

"We won't know anything for another couple of weeks. Mom says it's a long shot." It sounded like I was talking about a lottery ticket.

"Still, wouldn't it be great if you could? I mean, that'd be huge. Like saving a life. You'd probably end up being so close to her." Toni sounded almost envious.

I pictured my blood filling the glass tube, the way the level of dark liquid had risen so fast. Something shifted uneasily inside me as I thought about Toni's words. Despite Mom's cautions, I had this weird conviction that I was going to be a match, but I didn't feel good about it. My reasons for wanting to help were all twisted up and wrong. I wanted to help because, despite not wanting to like Mark, I still wanted him to like me.

And—this was the really awful part—I kept having these stupid fantasies in which Mark cried and said how grateful he was, and there was an article about us in the local paper, and kids at school came up and talked to me and were all impressed, like I was some kind of hero. My face and ears burned just thinking about it. "I probably won't match," I said quickly.

Toni shrugged, losing interest. "I liked Mark. Are you going to see him again?"

I stepped squarely in a pile of leaves at the edge of the sidewalk, expecting a dry brittle crunch. Instead, the leaves felt slick and mushy under my feet. "I don't know."

"You always say that. '*I don't know.*'"

I looked at her, startled. "Do I?"

"Always. *I don't know, I don't know*. It's like…like your mantra or something."

"I don't—I mean, I don't mean to."

"You should try to act more confident. It's not very attractive, the way you're so, you know, so insecure."

"I'm not." I felt like she'd just punched me in the stomach. "Anyway, you're the one who's acting different lately. Why are you being such a bitch?"

Toni spun toward me, eyes wide; then she looked away. "I'm…you're right. I'm sorry, Dylan."

There was a long silence. I wondered if we were going to have another fight, or if it was already over. For the first time ever, I wondered how much longer we'd be friends. There was an awful sinking feeling in my belly at the thought. I couldn't imagine not having Toni in my life. I didn't think she had any idea how much I counted on her.

Toni nudged me. "Come on, we'd better get back."

There was a weird eerie light, almost a greenish tinge to the gray sky. The air felt heavy with dread and anticipation. I thought about mushroom clouds and fallout and nuclear winters, and listened to the sound of our footsteps as we retraced our steps back to the school.

TWENTY

At dinnertime on Friday, Julia arrived to pick up Mom. Julia always drove, which gave me one less thing to worry about. It was just as well, as Mom had downed at least three glasses of wine while I did her makeup.

"Jules! What do you think?" she asked, gesturing toward herself.

Julia was standing in our front hall, dressed in stiletto-heeled boots and a body-hugging black dress. "You look fabulous," she said.

Mom spun around. Her backless shirt showed off her tattoos, and Julia gave a low whistle. "Hot, hot, hot."

I made a face and Karma laughed.

"Dylan, did you do her makeup? For a girl who doesn't even wear makeup herself, you sure have a knack for it.

I should get you to do mine." Julia winked at me. "When I try to do that smoky-eyed look, I end up with raccoon eyes."

"Waterproof mascara," I said. "You look great though." She really did: bleached blond hair, red lipstick and serious curves. "Very Marilyn Monroe."

"You girls behave," Mom said, and she and Julia departed arm in arm.

"Have fun," I said.

I felt a pang of something like jealousy as I waved goodbye. Toni and I used to be like that, before Finn showed up. Mom and Julia had both had plenty of boyfriends, but it seemed like they both understood that while the boyfriends would come and go, their friendship was forever.

I stuck a couple of veggie burgers in the microwave, pressed Start and backed away to wait. Microwave ovens made me nervous. I figured in ten years we'd find out that they caused MS or Alzheimer's or something.

"Is one of those for me?" Karma asked.

"Uh-huh." The microwave beeped, and I extracted the steaming brown discs and dropped them onto slices of whole-wheat bread. "Dinner is served."

Karma squirted ketchup onto hers and mine. "It's sort of quiet without Amanda here."

"She's only been gone a few minutes," I said. It wasn't like we weren't ever home alone. I knew what she meant though. It felt different, knowing Mom would be gone all weekend. The small apartment seemed bigger and somehow less familiar.

Karma carried our plates into the living room, and I flipped on the TV.

"Dylan, come on. Not the *news*."

"Shhh." A very thin blond woman was saying something about an oil spill in Howe Sound, north of Vancouver. The screen flashed to a picture of a mustached man, a Coast Guard representative.

"Dylan!"

"Shut up, Karma."

"An estimated sixty tons of fuel has been spilled," the man was saying, his voice guarded and cautious. "There has been some impact on an environmentally sensitive marsh."

"This is *awful*." I turned up the volume.

"Yeah, but us listening to it isn't going to help." Karma grabbed for the remote.

I held it up above my head.

"We don't have any official confirmation of numbers or the type of wildlife affected…"

Karma sat down on the couch and took a bite of her veggie burger. "Can we at least check if there's anything good on?"

"Crews are working furiously to contain the spill, but high winds are driving the oil along the bird-populated waterways…"

I sighed and tossed the remote to her. "Sometimes I think we're all crazy. We're destroying the planet, and no one seems to care."

Karma clicked through a reality show and a Mazda commercial. *Zoom zoom zoom.* "They said they were trying to clean it up. If no one cared, it wouldn't even be on the news."

"If people really cared, these things wouldn't keep happening." I poked my finger at the ketchup puddled on my burger. "Everything's so messed up."

"Ha. I love this show." Karma leaned back and took another bite.

Some stupid sitcom. I watched her chewing contentedly. "I've got some people coming over later," I said.

"You do? Who, Toni?"

"Yeah, Toni and a couple of others."

Karma kept her eyes on the TV. "Whatever." Then she sat up and turned to look at me. "Your boyfriend? Right? I bet you invited your boyfriend."

"A couple of people, all right? It's not really any of your business."

"Bet you don't want Amanda to know."

I narrowed my eyes at her. "Is that a threat?"

"I'm just saying."

"Okay, fine. Yes, Jax is coming. And no, you don't need to mention that little fact to Mom."

"You're so lucky. I wish I was sixteen."

I sighed. I wished I was still eleven.

❧

Karma and I did the dishes. I washed, Karma dried, and no one put away. We just piled them on top of the ever-growing stack of clean dishes on the counter. Every once in a while, if Mom was planning on cooking something and needed the counter space, she'd put the dishes in the cupboards, but most of the time, no one bothered.

Karma nodded at the line of dried-out cactuses on the window ledge above the sink. "Poor things," she said.

"I know." They were Mom's, but I felt guilty every time I looked at them.

"It's like Death Row," she said. "Get it? Death Row?"

"Yeah, ha ha." My stomach clenched. Now I was going to think about that every time I looked at those cactuses. "We should just throw them out."

"They're Amanda's."

"They're dead." I picked up the cactuses, and one by one I banged them on the edge of the compost bin, so that the cactuses and soil came loose and fell on top of the scraps of vegetables and the coffee grounds. "And now they're gone."

The doorbell rang, and without looking at Karma, I ran down the stairs to answer it.

Toni was already in the hall, kicking off her boots and hanging her dripping raincoat on a hook. "It's disgusting out," she said. "I *walked* over. I'm soaked."

She was wearing a lacy black top and low-rise skinny jeans that showed off her hip bones and flat stomach. A silver ring twinkled at her navel. I felt a flicker of jealousy; not at her body, exactly, but at her ease with it. There was no way I could wear something like that and feel at all comfortable.

"You look great," I told her.

"Thanks." She grinned and opened her backpack. "I got three movies. Whaddaya think?"

Two comedies and an action flick. "Sure. Fine."

She followed me up the stairs. "Finn can't come; he has to work. But look what I brought instead." She rummaged in her bag and pulled out a bottle of peach Schnapps.

I felt a twisting in my stomach. If I hadn't invited Jax, it could have been just me and Toni. We'd just got to the top of the stairs when the doorbell rang. "I'll get it," I said. "Go put some music on, if you can find anything decent."

It was Jax. He hung his leather jacket beside Toni's raincoat and pulled me toward him. "Good to see you."

His arms circled my waist and held me close. I looked up at him and let him kiss me. His face was cold and his breath tasted like beer. I wondered if I would still like him if he had a different face. A less perfect face. If he had acne, or sticking-out ears, or a funny-looking nose.

Probably not, I thought uncomfortably. I squirmed away from him. "Come on. Toni's here too."

He followed me upstairs, his fingers threaded through the belt loops at the back of my jeans. "I didn't come here to see Toni," he said.

⟡

In the kitchen, Toni was mixing Peach Schnapps with orange juice from the fridge. She handed a glass to me and offered another to Jax.

He made a face. "You have any beer?" He opened the fridge, grabbed a beer—one of the ones Scott left—and cracked it open.

In the living room, the volume of the TV suddenly dropped to a soft murmur. I could practically feel Karma's big ears twitching.

"Toni got some movies," I said.

"Cool." Jax yawned. "Jeez. I'm tired. Worked practically every night this week." He winked at me. "Except one."

I felt myself blush and looked away. The doorbell rang again.

"That'll be Jessica and Ian," Toni said. She downed her drink in one gulp and disappeared down the stairs.

Jax watched her leave. "Your friend likes to have a good time, huh?"

I wondered if he was wishing I was more like her. "Yeah. She's a lot of fun. We've been friends since we were kids."

"I moved around too much for that," Jax said. "Changed school every couple of years. So, you know, you make friends and say goodbye. No point in getting too attached."

"You think you'll stay here? To finish high school?"

"Oh yeah, sure. Probably." He rummaged in his bag. "I brought some weed. Wanna—?"

I clapped my hand over his mouth and whispered in his ear. "My little sister is in the living room, listening to every word."

"Oh. I mean, I was going to do some weeding…um. But it rained."

I giggled. "Weeding, huh?"

"Right. Maybe you could help? I mean, if it stops raining?" He pulled out a pack of rolling papers.

I glanced at the flour jar where Mom kept her stash. She didn't know that I knew about it, but she's had the same hiding place for at least five years. Toni and I took some a few times, just to try it, when we were thirteen. It didn't do a whole lot—just made me kind of relaxed and a bit hungry. I didn't really see why people were so into it, but if I had to do something, I'd rather smoke up than drink.

I looked at Jax and grinned. "Want to come to my room?"

"Oooh baby."

"Shut up."

He laughed. "Lead the way."

TWENTY-ONE

My bedroom window was the old-fashioned kind that slides open from the bottom up. Jax and I knelt on my bed and leaned out, cupping our hands over the joint and blowing the smoke into the rain. I kept thinking about what he'd said about Toni and wondering if he thought I was too serious and too uptight.

Jax butted out the tiny end of the joint on the window ledge and banged the window closed. His hair was hanging over his face, dripping water onto my pillow. I could hear voices from down the hall. I pushed my own wet hair back behind my ears and giggled. "The others are going to wonder what we've been doing."

Jax grinned. He leaned back against the wall and pulled me toward him. His lips were cold on mine, his teeth hit mine awkwardly and his mouth tasted like smoke. I pulled away. "Not now. Come on, everyone's in the kitchen."

"Okay, okay."

Whatever we'd just smoked must have been stronger than what my mom smoked. My thoughts were little bubbles that kept popping before they were fully formed. I giggled all the way to the kitchen. Jax's hand rested at my waist, his fingers laced through my belt loops.

"Where'd you two disappear to?" Toni took two more of Scott's beers out of the fridge, handed them to Jax and Ian, and poured another inch of Schnapps into her own glass.

"Nowhere."

Jessica grinned at me knowingly, and I racked my brain for a topic of conversation. "Um, so did you hear about that oil spill? In Howe Sound?"

Everyone looked at me blankly. Toni laughed and took a swig of Schnapps and OJ. "Dylan, you slay me."

"I'm…" I was about to say I was serious but bit off the words just in time. "You guys want to watch a movie?"

❧

My brain wasn't working properly at all. Toni had put on a comedy, which looked like it should require about three brain cells to watch, and I couldn't follow the story at all. I was definitely stoned. Jax drummed out the soundtrack on my thigh, his fingers tapping lightly. My leg felt like it belonged to someone else.

Toni was squished against my other leg, the three of us squeezed together on the couch. Ian was sitting straight-backed and cross-legged on the floor, and Jessica was curled up beside him. On the TV screen, a pregnant woman was sobbing wildly. She appeared to be at a funeral. Toni suddenly got up and dashed down the hall, muttering something about the washroom. I snuck a sideways glance at Jax. He was watching the movie, his eyes and teeth gleaming in the light of the television.

Karma kept staring at me from across the living room. She was making me nervous. I felt like I was setting a bad example or something, even though I wasn't really doing anything at all. Jax's hand was still on my leg, and I could feel Karma watching his every move.

I wasn't sure how much time had passed, but the funeral was over and the movie characters were in a restaurant now. It seemed like Toni had been gone for ages. I put my hand over Jax's. "Be right back," I whispered.

I finally found Toni in my bedroom. She was sitting on the floor, crying.

"What's wrong?" I asked, horrified. Toni never did things like this. Besides, she'd seemed fine earlier, and nothing could have happened since then.

She didn't answer. I grabbed a Kleenex from the box on my dresser and knelt beside her. "Talk to me, Toni."

Toni studied the Kleenex for a minute like she'd never seen one before. Finally she took it and blew her nose into it. Her mascara was streaked down her cheeks in two dirty rivers. "This sucks. I'm sorry."

"It's okay. Really." The sick selfish part of me felt good that Toni needed me for once. Lately it seemed like I'd been the one having all the problems.

"I hate girls who get drunk and cry at parties." Toni gave a shaky laugh that turned into a sob.

"This isn't a party," I reminded her.

She sounded as if she was choking. "Dylan, you're so weird sometimes."

"I know."

We sat side by side on the floor. From down the hall, I could hear voices and laughter from the TV. "Please tell me what's wrong," I whispered.

Toni wrapped her arms around her knees and hugged them to her chest. She stared down at the carpet for a long moment before she turned her head to the side and met my eyes. "I think I'm pregnant."

"Oh. Oh, Toni."

"Yeah."

The wind was blowing the rain sideways, and it splatted in big heavy drops against my window. *Tap tap tap.*

Jax's fingers against my thigh, the sound of my thought bubbles popping. I had an awful urge to giggle. "I'm stoned," I told Toni apologetically. "If I seem odd…"

"Yeah, I kind of noticed."

There was a long silence and I tried to concentrate. "Jeez. So, are you sure? I mean, you could just be late, right?"

"I'm never late."

"How late are you?"

"Two weeks. At first I kept thinking maybe I'd just mixed up my dates, or, I don't know. Hoping I'd start my period. Trying not to think about it." She looked at me. "But tonight I started to feel kind of queasy. And my boobs hurt. That's bad, right?"

I'd never even been a week late. Not that I had a reason to keep track. "That sucks, Toni. I mean, that really, really, really…"

"Sucks. Yeah."

We sat in silence for a moment. I couldn't imagine how freaked out I'd be if it was me. I felt like I was in a movie or something, like this wasn't our real lives. "I guess if you really are pregnant, you'll have an abortion, right?"

Toni looked away. "I don't know. I guess, probably."

"What other choice is there?"

"Duh."

She couldn't be serious. "You can't have a *baby*."

"Why can't I?"

"Well, because. Because you're sixteen." I couldn't believe she was even considering it. "What does Finn say?"

There was a long, long silence. Finally Toni sniffed a bit, wiped her nose again, and rubbed her hands across her eyes, leaving black smeary circles around them. "I haven't told him."

"You haven't? Why not?"

"I haven't told anyone. Just you."

"Yeah, but—well, you have to tell Finn. I mean, it's kind of his problem too, right?"

She gave a snort. "Seems like my problem to me."

"It's his fault as much as yours." I winced. "I don't mean *fault*, like I'm blaming anyone. I mean"—I searched for the word in my fuzzy brain—"responsibility."

"Yeah, I know."

I thought about Mom, finding out she was pregnant at the same age we were now, and keeping it secret. "I think you should tell him."

"I know. I *know*."

"But, Toni, what are you doing with him if you can't even talk to him about something this huge?"

"I love him," she said. "And I don't want to do this to him, you know? I don't want to mess up his life."

"How come you're acting like this is all on you?"

Toni shook her head. "Forget it, Dylan. I'll figure it out." She stood up slowly, and curved her lips in an imitation of her usual easy grin. Her freckles looked dark as pepper scattered against her pale skin. "God, I feel sick. I just threw up."

"Maybe it's the Schnapps?" If Toni was pregnant, she shouldn't be drinking. I opened my mouth to say something, and then closed it again. There was no way Toni could have a baby. I couldn't imagine it.

"It's not the Schnapps." Toni crossed my room to peer into the mirror. "Dammit. Look at me, I'm a mess." She spat on the corner of a fresh Kleenex and rubbed at the streaks of mascara on her face.

I looked at her tummy, smooth and drum-taut above her low-rise jeans. A girl at our school got pregnant last year and decided to have the baby. We hadn't been close friends, but still, it had been weird watching her belly swell up and listening to her chatter about baby showers and changing tables and strollers—like she'd crossed over some invisible line and become forever different from the rest of us. I couldn't imagine that happening to Toni.

"Are you going to tell your mom?" I asked.

"I don't know. I guess I'll have to if I don't have an abortion."

"If you want me to go with you, like to a doctor or something…"

She frowned. "My family doctor would tell my mom. They've known each other forever. I mean, he's been my doctor since I was *born*. There's no way I can tell him."

"So what are you going to do? You can't just ignore it."

"I can't do anything tonight anyway." Toni tugged on her bangs to straighten them and made a disgusted face as they sprang back up again. "Come on. We'd better get back to the others."

⌒

Jessica, Ian and Jax had paused the movie and were playing a card game on the living-room table. Karma had disappeared to her room.

Jax looked up. "What is it with girls always going to the washroom together?"

I tried not to look at Toni. "Ha ha. How come you stopped the movie?"

"Because we're thoughtful and considerate. We didn't want you to miss out." Jax grinned at me.

"Oh, listen to him. Someone wants to get laid." Jessica laughed.

Jax shrugged, still grinning. "I'm a guy, okay? What can I say?"

Everyone laughed, but Toni's laughter came a few seconds too late. "Think I need a refill," she said, holding up her empty glass.

I followed her into the kitchen and watched her pour a drink that was more Schnapps than orange juice.

Toni wouldn't like it, but I had to say something. I put my hand on her arm. "Toni. Look, if you really think you might have a…" I couldn't say *baby*. I lowered my voice to a whisper. "If you aren't going to have an abortion, then you shouldn't be drinking."

"You can't be serious." She shook my arm off and looked at me, eyebrows raised. "I've got more immediate things to worry about than some hypothetical baby's IQ."

"But it's not hypothetical. I mean, if you have it, it'll be a person."

Toni sat down on a kitchen stool and took a long drink, her eyes watching me over the rim of the glass. Finally she set the glass down. "You were pretty enthusiastic about me getting rid of it a few minutes ago. Abortion is okay, but I can't have a drink? Jeez, that makes a lot of sense."

I struggled to think it through, my ideas fuzzy but nonetheless certain. "Look, Toni, I think it's up to you whether you want to have this baby, okay? And to be honest I hope you decide not to. But if you do, you're responsible for it, right? And you can't go…" I gestured at the now half-empty glass. "You can't go doing stuff that'll mess the kid up."

Toni burst into tears. "I might not even be pregnant, okay. I don't *know*."

"I'm sorry." I sat there helplessly, wishing I'd just kept my mouth shut.

"Just go," Toni said. "Just go hang out with Jax and leave me alone."

I hesitated.

"I mean it, Dylan. Go."

I hesitated a moment longer, not wanting to leave her. Finally I turned away and left Toni sitting there staring at her drink.

Jax intercepted me at the kitchen door. "I was just coming to look for you." He peeked past me into the kitchen and lowered his voice. "What's up with her?"

"Nothing."

"Yeah? How about you show me your room again? I was thinking about"—he made an exaggerated show of looking around—"doing some more weeding. You know. If the rain stops."

I glanced back at Toni, who was still sitting with her glass in her hand and face turned away from us. I wanted to go to her, but her shoulders were shaking, and I knew she wouldn't want Jax to see her crying. So, not knowing what else to do, I followed him down the hall to my room.

TWENTY-TWO

Jax and I smoked another joint out my window; then we lay side by side in my bed, kissing and making out. I didn't know if it was the pot or if it was just me, but I felt disconnected from what was happening.

I leaned my forehead against his and wished I could read his mind. Just for a few minutes. Just to know how he really felt about me.

"Jax?"

"Yeah?"

"What are you thinking about?"

He pulled back slightly and looked at me. "Nothing."

I rolled away from him and lay on my back, staring up at the ceiling. That night at the beach, when he'd talked about his family, I'd thought maybe we could be closer.

Mostly though, he just kept pushing me away. Not physically, obviously, but when it came to getting to know him better. It was weird, to be touching like this and still feel so separate. Maybe he didn't trust me. Or maybe he just didn't think about things all the time, the way I did. Maybe he really was thinking nothing.

I couldn't imagine it. *How does a person think nothing? I wanted to ask him. Can you really do it? Just switch off that stream of images and words and worries?* It sounded like heaven to me.

"Jax?"

"Mmm hmm?"

I kept looking at the ceiling. Still the same number of dead bugs in my lampshade. "How come you wanted to get to know me? I mean, you said you asked someone my name, after that first class we had together. Why did you?"

He just laughed.

I turned my face toward him. "Seriously. I want to know."

"Because you were the hottest girl in the class. So are you going to give me shit for being sexist or something?"

I didn't think it was sexist exactly, but it seemed kind of shallow. Which I knew was totally unfair of me. I'd been interested in him because of his looks too. Still, I was disappointed. I don't know what I'd wanted him to say. "That's it? Just because you thought I was hot?"

"Mostly, yeah. Plus, I don't know. You didn't talk at all in class. I guess I thought you seemed sort of mysterious and sad or something."

"Probably just bored to death and trying to stay awake." I suddenly felt depressed.

Jax shifted his weight so he was laying half on top of me. He grinned at me and started to slide his hand under my shirt. His brown eyes were almost closed, his hand warm against my skin.

I quickly put my hand on top of his, holding it steady against my ribs. "Can you feel my heart beating?"

"Sure, I guess." He tried to move his hand up higher, but I held it still.

"Jax. If something happened…like if I got pregnant or something…could I, you know, count on you?"

He laughed. "That's not going to happen."

It wasn't an answer. I opened my mouth to say so, but he leaned in to kiss me. I pulled away. "Toni thinks she's pregnant."

"Seriously? Shit."

"Don't tell anyone." As soon as the words were out, I felt slightly sick. I shouldn't have told him.

"Shit. Finn must be shitting himself."

"He doesn't know."

Jax sat up and looked at me. "You're kidding."

"She doesn't want him to know." I propped myself up on my elbows.

"Yeah, but he has a right to know, don't you think? It's his baby as much as hers."

"It's her body though. And anyway, it's not a baby yet. It's just a few cells."

Jax shook his head, his jaw clenched tightly. "Don't give me that crap."

I pulled my shirt back down, tucked it into my jeans and sat up. "Christ. You can't be anti-choice."

"Don't tell me what I can or can't be." His voice was stiff and cold.

"Yeah, but come on, Jax. It's pretty basic, right? I mean, it's sort of a human-rights issue, you know?"

"Exactly," he said. "The baby should have some rights too."

"It's a fetus," I said. "Not a baby. It's the size of a bean. Besides, what if I got pregnant? I couldn't have a kid."

"I told you, that's not going to happen."

When I was younger, Mom used to volunteer at an abortion clinic, helping women get past the protesters who marched back and forth out front. I'd gone with her a bunch of times and could still picture the red angry faces and the shouting and jostling. "Damn right it won't," I said, and my voice came out thick and choked with tears.

We sat there in silence for a moment, the air too still and hot, the smell of pot smoke lingering, both sharp and sweet.

Finally Jax sighed. "Don't be like that. It's just, you know, my mom could've just aborted me. I told you what happened. Most people would've—"

"This isn't about you."

Jax's face tightened, his lips a thin hard line and a muscle twitching in his jaw. He stood up and walked out of my room without saying a word.

TWENTY-THREE

I sat there, feeling stunned. What the hell had just happened? I kept replaying the conversation and trying to make sense of it. I wished I wasn't stoned. My mind kept drifting and I couldn't figure anything out. Eventually I wandered down the hall to Karma's room.

She looked up from her book, surprised and wary. "Hi."

"Hi." I sat down beside her on the Little Mermaid comforter. She was too old for it really. Mom had bought it for her when she first came to live with us. "I just had a fight with Jax."

"Good."

"Good? I thought you wanted me to have a boyfriend."

She laid the book down on her pillow. *Big Blue Book of Bicycle Repair.* "Not him though."

"Why not?"

She just shook her head and didn't answer.

I looked at her more closely. "Karma? Have you been *crying*?"

Her shoulders hunched, and she turned away from me. I put a tentative hand on her bony back and wondered what to say. I couldn't even remember the last time Karma cried. She was one of the toughest people I knew. "Karma…please tell me what's wrong."

She pulled her knees up and pressed her face against them. After a few seconds she spoke in a muffled voice. "I know you guys were doing drugs."

I thought about denying it but decided not to. I hated it when people lied about stuff that was obvious. "Just smoking pot," I said. "It's no big deal."

"It is."

I couldn't see her face, but I could feel her shoulders shaking. "Why are you so upset? Is it because Amanda's away?"

"No." She turned back to look at me. The skin around her eyes was all red and puffy. "I told you why."

"Yeah, but come on…It's not like we were shooting heroin." I broke off abruptly. "God, Karma, I'm sorry. That was a dumb thing to say."

"It's okay. I mean, I know my mom had a problem with drugs. I just don't want you to…"

"I wouldn't. I mean, I hardly ever even smoke up." I made a face that was supposed to be reassuring. "Honest. I don't even like it much."

She nodded but didn't say anything.

"Look, if it would make you feel better, I won't do it anymore. Okay? Really, Karma. I promise." I looked at her anxiously. Toni and now Karma. Everyone was falling apart tonight.

There was a crash in the kitchen, and I stood up reluctantly. "I'd better go see…"

"Okay."

"Karma? I mean it. I won't do it anymore."

She nodded. "Good."

In the kitchen, Toni was wiping up a puddle strewn with broken glass. "Sorry," she muttered. "My fault. I just…" She gestured at the floor. "Dunno. Dropped my drink."

"It's okay. I mean, the glasses aren't anything special." I sat down on the floor. "I think Jax and I just broke up."

"Seriously? You guys seemed fine an hour ago."

"I know. It was totally stupid. We got in this argument about abortion, if you can believe it." I realized my mistake as soon as the words left my mouth.

She rocked back on her heels and stared at me. "You told him. Oh. My. God. You told him, didn't you?"

Crap. "Toni. I didn't mean to. It just sort of slipped out."

"That's just great." She tossed the cloth on the floor and stared at me, stony-eyed. "Just fucking great. Thanks so much, Dylan. So glad I can trust my best friend to keep a secret for a whole half hour."

"I'm really sorry." I started to cry. "Toni…"

"Forget it." She walked away, back out to the living room. "I'm leaving."

I followed her. "Don't go, Toni. Please."

She looked around the room. "I gotta go, guys."

"I'll give you a ride," Jax said.

I looked at him. "You're leaving too?"

He didn't meet my eyes. "I thought you'd want me to."

I didn't know what I wanted. Everything was a huge mess. "Fine," I said, feeling tired. "Go. Actually, maybe you'd better all just go."

They all gathered up their stuff and left, no one saying much at all. Toni barely looked at me. I wanted to tell her I was sorry that I'd told Jax her secret, but she didn't give me a chance to say anything. Jax barely looked at me either. I waited until I heard the front door slam shut; then I walked downstairs to lock it behind them. Instead I found myself stepping outside onto the porch. I watched Jessica and Ian get in their car, and Jax get onto his bike. He handed Toni his spare helmet, the one I usually wore, and she stepped onto the bike behind him.

Engines started up, headlights appeared in the dark street and seconds later they disappeared around the corner. I held on to the railing and leaned out, breathing in the night air and letting the rain fall on my face, cold and clean against my hot cheeks.

TWENTY-FOUR

When I finally crawled out of bed the next day, it was almost noon. It was barely even light in my room. Rain poured down, the wind howled and the sky was a dark, leaden gray. Last night came rushing back in all its stupid miserableness. I stared out the window. I was pretty sure that the thing with me and Jax was over. It felt like a failure and that bothered me a bit, but I didn't feel devastated or crushed or any of the things other girls said they felt when they broke up with guys. Mostly what I felt was an odd sense of relief. Until I thought of Toni and our fight and what I had done. There was a sick, heavy feeling deep in my stomach.

I picked up the phone and dialed her number. One ring, two, three...Her voice mail clicked on. "Hey, it's Toni.

Leave me a message and I'll call you back. Don't hang up…I have enough hangups already."

I hung up anyway. I couldn't believe I'd told Jax that she was pregnant. What the hell was wrong with me?

∽

Karma was lying on the couch in her pajamas, reading a book and eating toast. I could smell peanut butter. "Feels weird, doesn't it?" She spoke without lifting her eyes from her book. "Like a sick day or something."

I knew what she meant. It was too quiet in here, too dark outside. We had nothing to do and nowhere to go. I thought of the Dr. Seuss book Mom used to read to me when I was little: *So all we could do was just sit, sit, sit, sit.* "Yeah. It does."

I'd stayed up half the night, long after everyone had gone, messing around on my computer. Wikipedia said bone marrow was the soft tissue found in the hollow interior of bones. I'd never thought of bones as hollow.

I lifted my legs and hung them over the arm of my chair. Marrow, apparently, was also a kind of squash, a character in the X-Men comics, and the name of a sci-fi novel. I punched my thigh with my fist, hard.

It figured that bones weren't as solid as they looked. Nothing was. "I'm going out," I told Karma.

❧

I pedaled as hard as I could and made it through downtown and to the harbor in less than ten minutes. When I got off my bike, my legs felt as limp as cooked spaghetti and my hands were shaking. I pulled off my helmet and locked my bike to a No Parking sign in front Mark's hotel.

I didn't know what I was doing. All the way here I'd been having these conversations in my mind—well, not conversations exactly, because Mark never said anything. There was just all this stuff I wanted to say to him, running through my mind in a full-volume shout. Like, *What gives you the right to come here and mess up my life?* Stuff like that. But I didn't have a plan, and really, none of this was his fault, and now that I was standing outside his hotel it all seemed a bit stupid and melodramatic. I thought maybe I wouldn't go in after all. Maybe I'd just go home.

I turned my back on the building and watched a lone jogger running along the path near the waterfront. A seagull walked across the grass, pecking at some piece of food it had found. In the harbor, the roar of a seaplane engine briefly blotted out all the other sounds. I felt like lying down on the wet grass and going to sleep.

"Dylan?"

I turned around slowly. Mark was standing there, and beside him, holding his hand, was a little girl in a shiny yellow raincoat covered with drawings of big green frogs.

"We've just been for a walk," he said. "Dylan, this is Casey."

I stared at her for a long moment before I managed to drag my gaze back to him. "Um, I was just riding my bike."

"Were you looking for us? Have you been...?" He gestured at the hotel.

I shook my head. "No. Not exactly. I don't know."

We stood there for a long moment. I noticed that Casey had matching frog rain boots with googly eyes on the toes. "I guess I better, you know." I pointed at my bike. "Get going."

"Daddy?" Casey was tugging at Mark's sleeve. "You said we could go in the gift shop again."

She didn't look like me, I decided. Not at all. She must look like her mom.

"Do you want to come in?" Mark asked. "Perhaps you and Casey could play together a bit? If you wanted?"

Right. I bit off a sarcastic reply: *What am I, four?* "I should go."

Casey tugged at her dad's arm again. "Daddy, I want to go to the gift shop." Her mouth actually turned down at the corners, way down, like a little emoticon sad face.

"Are you sure? Casey has this great dollhouse. I bet she'd love to show you."

"How come you want me to hang out now?" I asked. I could see Casey watching me and chose my words carefully. "I already said I'd help out."

"Sorry." He looked uncomfortable. "I didn't mean to pressure you."

I shrugged. "I just wondered why, that's all."

"I'd like…" He cleared his throat. "I know I'm a bit preoccupied right now. With…" He nodded toward Casey. "But I know she'd enjoy showing it to you. And, well, you are my…like I told you before, I'd like to get to know you."

Daughter. He'd almost said it. "Fine," I said. "I'll come see her dollhouse. But I can't stay long." Then I blushed. It wasn't like he'd asked me to stay.

Casey's dollhouse was set up in the middle of their suite's living room, and it took up most of the available space. I'd never been into dolls or dollhouses, but I couldn't help being impressed. It was three stories high, wooden, with a shingled roof and gently curving circular staircases, and it was filled with perfect miniature furniture, rugs and curtains and everything.

"How did you get this on the plane?" I asked.

Mark laughed. "Lisa did that. It all comes apart, but it's a big job. Took her three hours to set it all up when they arrived."

"Wow." I picked up a tiny clawfoot tub. "This is amazing."

"That's a bathtub," Casey informed me.

She didn't have any hair, but other than that she didn't look sick at all. Her head was mostly covered in a cute knit hat, all pink and green stripes, and she was wearing a matching pink and green sweater. She had a round, fat-cheeked face and dimples when she smiled. She didn't look like a kid who was dying. "It's a great bathtub," I agreed. "I like the little feet."

Casey had moved on. She picked up a crib made of white painted wooden slats as narrow as toothpicks. "This is for the baby."

"Cute. Do you have one like that? At home, I mean?"

She looked at me disdainfully. "I sleep in a big-girl bed. Not a *baby* one."

"Of course you do."

Casey pointed at an upstairs bedroom. "This is the mommy and daddy's room. See?"

Two dolls lay side by side on a double bed covered with a white comforter the size of a Kleenex. All very Ken and Barbie. "Where's Casey's mom?" I asked Mark. "I mean, she's here too, right?"

He nodded. "She went out for a run."

I turned my attention back to the dollhouse. "You know, I bet you'd love Miniature World," I told Casey. "It's all, you know, scenes set up with miniature stuff."

"Min…Minner world?"

"Miniature World." I looked at Mark. He was still standing, leaning against the kitchenette counter. "It's this place downtown. Tourist attraction."

He nodded. "Let's go there."

"You too," Casey informed me.

"Oh, your dad will take you. You'll have fun with your dad." I looked at Mark for agreement, but instead he smiled at me.

"Why don't we all go? You and Casey could spend some time together."

I turned my back on Casey and lowered my voice, almost mouthing the words. "Does she know who… I mean, that we're…?"

He shook his head. "Not yet."

Casey tugged at my arm again. "What are you *saying*? What are you *talking* about?"

"Nothing."

"Don't whisper! It's rude."

Casey had two vertical lines between her eyebrows. Like mine. She'd have wrinkles by sixteen, too, if she didn't stop frowning. Except, of course, she might never make it past four. I swallowed a lump the size of a golf ball and thought of dark blood and hollow bones. "Sure," I said. "I'll come too."

❧

"I didn't realize you meant to go there now," I said to Mark while Casey struggled back into her raincoat and boots. "I mean, today."

He didn't take his eyes off Casey. "If all this has taught us anything, it's that today's the best time to do things. I'll call Lisa and tell her to meet us there." Then he looked at me as if he'd just remembered who he was talking to. "Sorry. Is today okay? Did you have to be somewhere else?"

"Not really. No." I cleared my throat. "I've got my bike. I'll meet you there."

Cycling down around the inner harbor with the cold rain hard against my face gave me a chance to think. I hadn't intended to meet Casey at all, and I hadn't even been sure I wanted to see Mark again, yet here I was, playing tourist with them. I tightened my grip on the handlebars and wondered why.

TWENTY-FIVE

"Miniature World: The Greatest Little Show on Earth," I said, reading the sign aloud for Casey. She grabbed my hand, which took me by surprise. I wasn't really a kid-person. Mom said I'd always preferred the company of adults, even when I was little. I'd never been the babysitting type. I'd spent time with Karma, of course, but she'd been eight by the time she joined our family. So I wasn't too sure how to act with Casey.

Fortunately, Miniature World was open—I hadn't thought to check before we came. It was pretty much deserted though, the summer's tourists long gone. Mark had called Lisa on her cell phone. Apparently she was already downtown and would be able to join us.

It was lucky it was so empty, since Casey was practically shrieking with excitement by the time we got inside. Lisa arrived, still in her running clothes and with her hair wet from the rain, just as we were paying for our admission. She was a short fair woman, a little plump, with shoulder-length hair and an anxious smile. She kept patting my shoulder in a weird, almost compulsive manner. "So nice to finally meet you. I've heard so much about you."

I raised my eyebrows. It seemed unlikely, given that Mark knew almost nothing about me.

She turned pink and patted my shoulder again. "We're very grateful." She glanced at Casey. "You know. For…"

"No big thing," I said quickly.

"Huge, for us."

"Yeah, well. You know. Hopefully…"

"Hopefully." Lisa nodded agreement. "We're all keeping our fingers crossed." She actually crossed her fingers for real and held them up, smiling at me.

"You bet." I crossed mine and held them up too, feeling like a complete dork.

She patted my shoulder again.

I moved away. Casey and Mark were already heading down the darkened hallway toward the exhibits. "Shall we?"

"Yes, yes. Sorry. I didn't mean to make you uncomfortable."

"No, it's fine." I practically sprinted down the hallway toward the others. "Casey! Wait up!"

We skipped past the miniature trains and the battle scenes and quickly found the room Casey wanted to see.

"World's largest dollhouses," I whispered, bending down to Casey's level. She was just tall enough to see the displays without an adult lifting her up.

I thought she'd rush from one dollhouse to the next, but she took her time, carefully studying each one. She was wide-eyed and silent, staring at the tiny rooms and pointing wordlessly at one tiny piece of furniture after another. "Pretty cool, huh?" I said.

Casey nodded. "Pretty cool."

It sounded funny coming from a little kid, and Lisa laughed. "That'll be her new phrase now, Dylan."

I wondered if she had noticed how much I looked like Mark. It must have been pretty strange finding out that her husband had a teenage daughter. I straightened up and looked at her. "She's a cute kid."

"She is." Lisa looked like she was going to say something more, but she just cleared her throat and patted my shoulder again.

I forced a smile and turned back to Casey. "Let's go look at the next one. Okay? See, it's got a baby's room, just like your dollhouse does. A nursery, they used to call it. These are olden-days houses, aren't they?"

Casey nodded. "They have horsies outside."

"Instead of cars. That's right."

"And buggies. Horsies and buggies." She looked up at me. "*I've* been on a horsey."

"Have you? Wow."

Casey nodded, her face serious. "A white horsey called Buddy."

"That's great," I said. For some reason, my chest was starting to feel all tight. It was too quiet in here, and too small. Narrow walkways and carpeted floors that absorbed sounds. Cavelike. I felt claustrophobic.

"Someday I'm going to have a horsey of mine own," Casey told me.

I nodded. "That'd be nice. What would you call it?"

Casey shrugged. "*I* don't know." Then she giggled. "*Silly.*"

"You'd call it Silly?"

More giggles. "No, *you're* silly."

"I am? Why?"

Casey didn't answer. She stared at the house for a long minute. "It's got a chimney."

I tried to focus, but my eyes were wet and everything was blurry. I blinked hard. "I have to go, Casey. I have to get home."

"Okay." She didn't look away from the house.

I stepped away from her. Mark and Lisa were standing behind us, just a few feet away, in an obvious attempt to give us space while still being able to hear every word. "I should get going," I said. "I don't want to leave Karma on her own for too long."

"Maybe we can get together again," Lisa said. "We're here for a few more days."

I stepped past them in the narrow aisle, not able to meet their eyes, barely able to see through the shimmery haze of my tears. "Maybe."

TWENTY-SIX

Karma and I were watching TV when Mom got home late on Sunday morning. I looked up and hit the Mute button on the remote. "Hey. How was the concert?"

"Good. Great. Unbelievable." Her smile faded when she looked at me. She gave me a hard-eyed stare. "Well. How was your weekend?"

I knew I looked terrible: I hadn't washed my hair, I had dark circles under my eyes and for some reason, my lips were all chapped. "Fine."

On the television, a field was sprouting a forest of windmills. "What're you watching?" she asked.

"A show about greenhouse gas emissions. Um, alternative energy sources." I switched the television off and passed the remote to Karma. "You want this? I have to make a couple of calls."

"You're going to make calls now? I just got home." Mom unzipped her jacket. "Aren't you going to tell me about your weekend?"

"Nothing to tell, really."

Karma switched to a reality TV show and turned the volume back on. Wannabe models tripped down a runway in heels high enough to break their spindly ankles.

"How can you watch this?" Mom asked. "It's total crap. Encouraging girls to obsess about their appearance." She shook her head. "Encouraging them to see other girls as competition. Life's hard enough without that."

Karma scowled. "I like it. Anyway, it's just a show."

"I'll be in my room," I said.

"What's wrong?" Mom put her hand on my arm.

I pulled away. "Nothing. I just don't feel like talking."

Karma tucked her feet beneath her and spoke without taking her eyes off the screen. "She broke up with her boyfriend."

"Oh. Dylan...I'm so sorry."

"I don't want to talk about it," I said. I glared at Karma. "Mind your own business, okay?" Then I took off for my room before I started to cry.

Within about two minutes, Mom knocked. She pushed my door open a few inches. "Can I come in?"

"Sure."

I was lying on my bed, pretending to read.

"Are you okay?"

I put my book down and rolled onto my side to face her. "I guess."

"Oh baby." Mom had that let–me-kiss-it-better tone in her voice. "I'm sorry. I guess you really liked him."

It was too much. I burst into tears and ducked my head, hiding my face.

Mom sat down beside me and put her hand on my back. "Oh baby. Pickle."

I was still angry with her, but at the same time I wanted to curl up and put my head on her lap like I used to when I was younger. "It's just…I don't think I liked him much anyway," I whispered.

"You didn't? But…"

"I don't even know why I went out with him. It was all just stupid."

She waited, rubbing my back lightly.

"Mom?" I caught my breath and shot her a fleeting sideways glance. "Do you think I'm, you know, normal?"

She snorted. "What's normal anyway?"

"Don't get all *new-age* on me. I mean *normal.* As in, like other people."

"I wouldn't want you to be like anyone else. But I don't think there's anything wrong with you." She frowned. "I mean, you're not…you're not hearing voices or anything like that?"

I shook my head impatiently and pulled away from her hand. I sat up. "No. Just, you know, with Jax. I never really wanted to…do anything." My cheeks were on fire and I couldn't even look at her.

"Sex, you mean?"

"Mom! God."

She laughed. "Lighten up, Pickle. Isn't it supposed to be parents who are uptight about discussing sex?"

She wasn't, that was for sure. I'd heard way too many details about her sex life.

"Maybe you just didn't like him enough. Or trust him enough or feel comfortable with him. Maybe he wasn't your type and you just weren't that attracted to him."

"He's good-looking. Everyone thinks so."

"So?"

"So maybe there's something wrong with me. That's all."

"Are you attracted to girls? Is that it?"

I thought of Toni and how often I wished it could just be the two of us, like it used to be. Growing old and living together and rescuing dogs. Was that being attracted to someone? Even if I never thought about kissing her or anything like that? I loved Toni. And I was sort of jealous of Finn. But…

"Because if you were, that'd be fine. I'd be cool with that."

"I'm not." My voice was almost a wail. "I wish I was though."

Mom's mouth twitched.

"Mom! If you laugh at me, I swear I'll never tell you anything again."

"Baby, I'm not laughing. But not everyone is having sex at sixteen, no matter what they say. I wish I hadn't." She was suddenly serious. "Well, I suppose I don't mean that, because I wouldn't have you, but you know what I mean."

"Not really." Mostly what I knew about her seemed to be lies.

Her eyes flicked away from mine for a brief moment. "If you don't want to have sex, then don't. Wait until you're ready. Believe me, it'll happen."

I wiped my eyes on my sleeve. "You think so?"

"I know so."

"Okay." I picked at a hangnail on my thumb. "So anyway."

"Change the subject?"

"Yeah. Please."

Mom stood up. "So, Seattle was good."

"Yeah?"

"The lead singer is a genius. He really is." She grinned. "And Julia got his phone number."

"Here we go." I rolled my eyes.

Mom laughed. "I'll go and unpack. And get something to eat. I'm starving."

"Mom?"

She paused, her hand on the door handle. "What?"

"Do you think we'll hear anything about the blood test this week?"

"No. Two weeks, they said."

I pulled my knees to my chest and wrapped my arms around them. "I sort of ran into Mark and Casey when I was out for a bike ride."

She spun back around to face me. "You ran into *Mark*? And you're just going to mention that little fact now? As a...as an afterthought? Jesus Christ, Dylan."

"It's no big deal." I was glad she didn't know about my earlier visit with Toni.

"Yes, it is. He's..."

"My father."

"Unfortunately, yes. That doesn't mean you have to sneak around behind my back—"

"Mom! I said I just ran into him, okay?" I hoped she wouldn't ask where I'd run into him. I didn't think telling her that I'd been hanging around his hotel would go over well.

"What did you talk about?" Her voice was strained.

"Nothing much. I don't really want to talk about him if you're going to be all psychotic about it."

"I'm not being...So did you meet Casey? How was she?"

"I don't know. Cute kid, I guess." My throat started to ache whenever I thought about her.

Mom's face closed tight and hard as a knot. "Remember what I said? It's not likely that you'll be a match."

"Not impossible though."

"No. It's not impossible."

"I don't want to let her down, you know? She's just a little kid. It's so unfair." I felt tears threatening, a wobble in my voice, and I clenched my teeth tightly to hold it all inside.

Mom's hand slid off the door handle. "You can't think of it like that. You wouldn't be letting her down."

"Whatever. I don't really want to talk about it. I just wanted to know when we'd hear the results."

She stood there for a minute, probably trying to figure out how to interrogate me about Mark without seeming psycho. She was so weird about him. I couldn't figure out if she hated him or if she was still sort of hung up on him. Finally she shook her head and left, closing the door behind her. I held the cool back of my hands against my hot cheeks and waited for my heart rate to return to normal. I hadn't intended to say all that stuff about Jax. It had just sort of come spilling out, a big ugly mess.

It was so embarrassing. Maybe she was right and it was no big deal. I mean, why *would* I want to have sex with a guy I didn't totally trust and didn't even really know?

On the other hand, after all the lies Mom had told me, I wasn't sure I should believe anything she said.

I eyed the telephone. I kept hoping Toni would call me first, even though I was obviously the one who needed to apologize. I knew Jax wouldn't call, and that was fine with me. When he'd driven off on his motorbike Friday night, he hadn't even looked back once. He'd been drunk too. I shouldn't have let Toni go with him. I picked up the phone, stared at it for a moment and put it back down.

Maybe it'd be better to go over to her place and talk in person.

TWENTY-seven

Toni's house was a short bike ride away, but it was like another world. My street was all duplexes and triplexes, with the occasional low-rent apartment building. The lawns were covered in dandelions. *Proudly Pesticide Free,* read one small hand-lettered sign. People drove old Honda Civics and Ford Escorts with bumper stickers that said things like *Free Tibet* and *Visualize Whirled Peas.* Toni's neighbors did not put bumper stickers on their Lexus suvs and their BMWs. The houses were old but not old as in scruffy, like mine. They were old as in heritage, beautifully restored, with freshly painted trim and manicured front lawns.

Toni opened her front door in flannel pants and a black UVic hoodie. Last night's black eyeliner was smudged under her eyes, and she looked like she'd just got out of bed.

I didn't know where to start. "Toni. Look, I wanted to say that I know I screwed up. You totally trusted me with…" I lowered my voice, not sure if her mom was around. "You know. What you told me. I don't know why I told Jax, but I'm so sorry. I wish I hadn't done it. If I could take it back…"

"You can't."

"I know." I swallowed. "I just blurted it out. As soon as I said it, I wanted to take it back."

She just looked at me, her face expressionless.

"Look, Toni. You're pretty much the most important person in my life, okay? I mean, you're my best friend. Jax is nothing. He's kind of a jerk, actually."

"I told you."

"Yeah, I know."

"You're better off without him, Dylan. He's an asshole."

I raised my eyebrows, startled at the forcefulness of her tone.

Toni leaned against the wall. "He gave me a ride home just so that he could hit on me."

"Oh." I wondered if she wanted to hurt me, if that was why she was telling me. "Did you…? Never mind. I don't want to know."

"Give me some credit," she said. "I told him to fuck off."

"You did?"

"Course I did. Come on! He knows I'm with Finn, but he figures I'm pregnant, so I must be easy." Toni's fists were clenched, her words coming hard and fast and aimed to sting. "What a loser. I don't get what you saw in him."

But it was me she was angry with, not Jax. I took a deep breath and tried to hold my voice steady. "I think I wanted to be like you. Like you and Finn. I wanted to be part of a couple like that." I chewed on my lower lip for a minute, trying to find a way to explain. "I guess I've been sort of jealous. It used to be just you and me, you know? And I'm happy for you, but sometimes…" I shrugged. "Sometimes it's hard. But I am so so so sorry I told Jax about your…you know. Do you hate me now?"

"I still can't believe you told him."

I shook my head helplessly. "I can't explain it, Toni. We smoked some weed. He wanted to fool around, and I asked him what he'd do, you know, if I got pregnant. And he wouldn't listen. He wouldn't take me seriously. And it just sort of slipped out." I started to cry. "Please don't be mad at me forever."

Toni shrugged. "I'm not exactly mad. I don't know if I can trust you anymore, that's all."

"You can. I promise. Toni, whatever you want to do, I'll help you. If you'll still let me. I mean, if you want to get an abortion, or keep the baby, I'll be there for you."

"I know that, stupid." She started to cry.

"Toni? It'll be okay. It will."

She shook her head, cheeks wet with tears.

I grabbed her arm, pulled her out onto the porch and pulled her front door shut behind her. "Okay? Now your mom can't hear us. Talk to me. Please?"

Toni sat down on the top step, rubbed her hands over her face and gave a shuddery sort of sigh. "I got my period this morning. I'm not pregnant."

"Toni! That's so great. I mean, so really, truly, incredibly great." I sat down beside her. "How come you're crying?"

She sniffed and wiped her eyes on her sleeve. "I don't know." She looked at me and immediately started crying again. "Relief, I guess. Or hormones."

"I've been such a wreck," I whispered. "I figured you'd never speak to me again."

"It'd serve you right." She leaned her head on my shoulder. "I'm such an idiot, Dylan. God. What if I had been pregnant?"

"What do you think you would have done?"

"I don't know. I thought about how it might be, having a baby. And part of me was almost excited about it, you know?"

"Nope."

"Come on. Buying baby clothes, having this little person who'd love me no matter what."

I rolled my eyes. "Please."

"I know." She rested her elbows on her drawn-up knees. "Finn would have wanted me to get an abortion. I mean, I know he'd have said it was my decision, but still, he wouldn't have wanted a baby."

"Oh, Toni." I put one arm around her shoulders. "I can't blame him."

She made a funny gulping sound, cleared her throat, ran her sleeve across her eyes. "I just don't think he's ready to be a father, you know?"

"No kidding. He's, what, seventeen?"

She gave me a sideways look. "Your parents were our age."

"Yeah, and look how that worked out." I felt a weird pang of compassion for my mom, and a sudden curiosity. Had it been like this? My mom and her friend Sheri, trying to decide what to do?

"I was scared that if I had an abortion, I might regret it later. But then I thought about your mom," Toni said. "And, no offense, but having a baby so young kind of screwed up her life, didn't it? I mean, I want to go to university and all that."

I shrugged. "My mom always says she never regretted it."

"Well, sure. She has to say that, doesn't she?" Toni tucked her hair behind her ears, where it stayed for about one second before springing free. "Anyway, I decided I could have regrets either way. I mean, if I had a baby and regretted it? That'd be way worse than regretting an abortion."

"Yeah. Yeah, for sure." We were quiet for a moment. A bunch of crows swooped overhead and landed nearby, pecking at the grass and cawing raucously.

"I'm so glad I don't have to make that decision," Toni said.

"God, yeah. Plus, imagine telling your mom."

"Believe me, I've been imagining it."

I thought about Toni's mom. She was very nice, but she was also very conventional. Conservative, even. In her world, teenagers did not have sex. They definitely did not get pregnant.

"I wish I had your mom, sometimes," Toni said.

"She would totally freak out if I got pregnant." I thought about the weird sex conversation I'd had with my mom that morning. It had been embarrassing, but I had to admit she'd been cool. No heavy warnings about being careful or taking precautions. I liked to think that she figured I knew all that—we'd had the Big Sex Talk when I was about twelve—but who knew. Probably she was secretly relieved that her daughter's biggest worry was that she might never want to have sex.

Toni got up. "I'm starving. You want to come in and have some lunch with me?"

"Okay."

She tugged on the door. "Nice one, Dylan. You've locked us out."

"Oops. Sorry. I didn't want your mom to hear us." I gestured at the house. "Can't you just knock?"

"My mom's not even home, you idiot. And I'm in my pajamas." She started to laugh. "You better take me to your house and feed me. Otherwise I really will be pissed at you."

I gestured to my bike. "Hop on the back, if you want." She grinned and we both got on.

"We haven't ridden double in years," Toni said as we set off, wobbling slightly.

I pedaled harder. "Yeah. It's coming back to me though. You know what they say… 'It's like riding a bike.'"

"Har har har."

We rode in silence for a while. My hands were freezing, but the sky, for once, was blue. A bank of low dark clouds ringed the horizon, leaving a clear patch right over town. It was often like that here. Something to do with the ocean and mountains. I listened to the zinging noise of the bike tires on the still-wet road and felt calmer than I had in ages.

Toni and I were okay again. Jax was history. Everything was going to be okay. And I just knew my bone marrow would be a match for Casey.

It had to be.

TWENTY-EIGHT

On Friday morning, I woke up feeling anxious. I lay in bed, sorting through the haze of sleep and dreams and trying to figure out why. There were too many things to be worried about lately. A cloud of anxiety drifted at the edges of my mind, ominous but undefined. I'd dreamed about Casey, that she'd been flying back to Ontario and the plane had crashed. I sat up and rubbed my hands over my face, trying to erase the dream from my mind.

It had been nine days ago since I'd had the blood test. Five days to go. I hadn't seen Casey or Mark again. Mark had told me to call them, but I hadn't, and he obviously wasn't interested enough to make a call himself. For all I knew, they were back in Ontario already.

Anyway, I wasn't expecting to hear from them. So when the phone rang while I was eating breakfast, I assumed it was Toni and ran to answer it.

"Dylan? It's Mark. Ah, is Amanda there?"

She was in the living room, but I didn't want to be the last to find out. "Not right here. So…did you get the test results already?"

"Not yet."

I wondered why he was calling. Not to chat with me, clearly. The back of my neck tingled, like little electric shocks running down my spine. "So, um, I guess you're back in Ontario now?"

"No." He hesitated.

I figured he was wondering whether to call back later and talk to Mom. "So what's up? How's Casey?"

"Actually, that's why I'm calling. She's not too well. She's been admitted to hospital." He cleared his throat. "She's at the General. I was wondering if you'd like to come and see her. She really enjoyed meeting you. She's talked a lot about it."

I wanted to ask if she was going to be okay, but something stopped me. "She sure liked those dollhouses," I said instead.

"She sure did."

There was a long pause. "Um. I think I hear Mom," I told him. "I'll just go get her."

I took the phone into the living room. Mom was lying on the floor in some weird yoga pose. I handed her the phone. "It's Mark."

She swung her legs back to a more normal position and took the phone. "Mark? Hi."

I hung around, trying to listen in, but all Mom said was stuff like, *Yeah*, *Uh-huh*, *Okay*, *Oh no*, *I see*, et cetera, et cetera. So I had no idea what the conversation was about. I pulled at a hangnail on my thumb until the skin tore and a tiny droplet of blood squeezed out. I stared at it and wondered how they tested blood. Something about HLA markers, from what I'd read online, but I didn't really know what that meant.

I remembered Lisa's crossed fingers and found myself crossing mine tightly. The gesture didn't feel foolish this time. I pictured Casey's round face as she looked at the dollhouses, and hoped as hard as I could that I could help her.

Even if Mark never did want to spend time with me. Even if no one ever knew about it. Even if the doctors had to stick needles in every bone in my body.

Mom finally put down the phone and turned to me. "I guess you know that Casey's sick."

I hunched on the couch and wrapped my arms around my knees. "What's wrong with her?"

"Mark said she had a fever and was throwing up, so they took her to Emergency. Because, you know, they were worried..."

"Is it the cancer? It's come back?" Mark had said that Casey's remission probably wouldn't last very long, but it hadn't occurred to me that she might relapse before we even knew whether I could help.

She gestured helplessly. "They don't know. I mean, yeah, that's what they're worried about."

"But throwing up...I mean, lots of kids throw up. Right? It could be just stomach flu or something."

Mom sat down on the couch beside me and tried to put an arm around my shoulder, but I stiffened and pulled away. I hate being touched when I'm upset, and Mom's always doing it.

"Listen, Pickle. They don't know. So yes, it could just be a virus."

"But they don't think so. Mark doesn't think so, does he?" My voice wobbled.

"He's hoping that's all it is, but he's scared and..." Mom hesitated.

"What? What were you going to say?"

"Oh, baby...Casey's blood counts are down. Her platelets, Mark said, and something called neutrophils."

"They're a type of white blood cell." I wrapped my arms

around myself. I'd read about all this online. "Not the ones she has cancer in. Another kind."

Mom gave me an odd look. "Well, that can indicate a relapse. But it's possible that it's due to a virus too. They don't know for sure yet."

"I have to be a match," I whispered. "I have to be."

Mom didn't say anything.

"Can I stay home?"

"Sitting by the phone isn't going to make any difference. Anyway, school will help take your mind off all this." She hesitated. "I'll pick you up after school. I think it'd be a good idea for you to visit her. I'm sure she'd like that."

I stared at my mother for a minute, trying to read beneath the words, see past all the lies she'd told me. I dropped my eyes to her wrist, but the red and green of the hummingbird was hidden beneath her sleeve.

"You better go," she said. "You don't want to be late."

TWenTY-nine

After school, I stood outside beside my bicycle, waiting
for Mom. She'd arranged for us to go see Casey. No one
had said it, but I had a feeling this was a goodbye visit, in
case Casey didn't make it. There just seemed to be this
urgency about it. No one had consulted me or asked if I
wanted to go.

I didn't.

Toni was walking toward me and I waved.

"Hey. What are you doing?"

"Mom's picking me up."

She raised her eyebrows. "How come? You okay?"

I never let Mom drive me to or from school,
on principle. "We're going to see Casey," I said reluctantly.
"She's in the hospital."

"Jeez. Is it…serious?"

"Dunno. I guess it might be."

"Huh. That sucks." She gave me a long look. "I guess you haven't heard anything yet, about the bone-marrow thing."

I shook my head. "It's so weird. I feel like it'll be my fault if I'm not a match. You know? If she, you know…"

"Doesn't make it?"

"Yeah."

"It won't be your fault."

I shrugged irritably. "I *know* that."

There was a long silence. Toni played with a piece of tape on my bicycle handlebars, and Mom's car came rattling along and pulled to a stop beside us. I didn't want to go. "Sorry I'm being a bitch," I muttered. "Um, you know. You're my best friend. You're important to me."

"I love you too." She laughed. "Goof."

Toni helped me put my bike on the bike rack and waved goodbye as I slid into the passenger seat and buckled my seat belt. I watched her as we drove away, and wished I was still standing there on the sidewalk beside her. Mom drove quickly, trying to get onto the highway before the worst of the rush-hour traffic out of town. I turned on the radio so that we wouldn't have to talk. I felt trapped and panicky, my heart racing so fast I thought it'd burst right out of my chest. I dug my nails into my palms and clenched my teeth so tightly that my jaw started to ache.

I couldn't do it. I couldn't go see her.

Not if she was dying.

I couldn't even stand to think about it. It wasn't even about Casey, really. It wasn't about how sad it was that a little kid was sick, or about her being my half sister. I just couldn't stand thinking about death. Being *reminded* of it. The certainty of death changed every-thing. What difference did it make how far off it was? If death was the inevitable outcome, how could anything else really matter?

"Mom." I started to cry. "I don't want to visit."

"What? Why not?"

I just shook my head. "Please don't make me. I can't do this." A blue sign with a big letter H on it flashed past, and I started to cry harder.

She took her foot off the gas and the car slowed down. "Are you sure, Dylan?"

"I'm sure."

"Dylan..." Mom shook her head. "Fine. I'll take you home and I'll call Mark on his cell."

She was probably disappointed in me. Casey would be disappointed too. But I just couldn't do it. Not yet. Maybe later—if I found out that I was a match and I could do something to help her—maybe then I'd visit.

When we got home, I retreated to my room. I didn't want to look at Mom's tight lips and wonder when she was going to ask me something. I could tell she was dying to. If she wasn't so big on respecting privacy, she'd probably already be interrogating me. I figured I'd better stay out of her way and remove the temptation.

I mucked around on the computer for a while, reading about neutrophils and platelets and leukemia. I couldn't make sense of a lot of it. After about half an hour, Karma hammered on my door.

"What?"

She slipped into my room. "Guess who's here?"

I glanced up, saw her wide grin and quickly minimized the window on the computer screen so she wouldn't see what I was reading. "How the hell would I know? Santa Claus?"

"Better. Scott."

"Really?"

"Yup. And I think they're back together." She lowered her voice, even though there was no way Mom could hear. "They're holding hands."

"Huh."

"You're not upset? Because I know you don't like him as much as I do."

"He's all right," I said. "As long as I don't have to see them making out on the couch again."

Karma wrinkled her nose. "Yeah. Gross."

"Is he staying for dinner?"

"Looks like it. He's helping her cook."

I didn't feel like sitting at a table with them all. On the other hand, Mom probably wouldn't ask me questions if Scott was there.

❦

I had to admit one thing: Scott sure could cook. Mom's repertoire was pretty much limited to pizza, frozen lasagna and mac 'n' cheese, but Scott was turning out to be Mr. Gourmet. I took a tortilla and began piling it with red peppers, mushrooms, onions, and cheese. Beside me, Karma had stuffed hers with so much steak that she couldn't get it to close.

"That's enough protein to feed a small village for a week," I told her under my breath.

She crossed her eyes at me and took a messy bite.

Mom and Scott weren't paying attention to either of us. They were knocking back shots of tequila and sneaking kisses when they thought we weren't watching. I pulled a piece of tortilla off my fajita and chewed it slowly.

Maybe Karma was right and Scott wasn't so bad. I wasn't convinced yet—but even I had to admit Mom seemed a whole lot happier when he was around.

∾

Sunday was a cold, clear blue-sky day, and Karma and I went for a bike ride together. We cycled up to Thetis Lake and sat at a picnic table, watching half a dozen dogs romping on the beach. My heart was beating hard from the last long hill up to the parking lot, and my face felt frozen.

Karma pulled off her helmet, put it down on the bench and turned to face me. "So. How come you're not going to see Casey?"

"Dunno."

"Do you think she's going to...? You know."

"How would I know?"

Karma bent down and picked up a rock. She rolled it in her hand for a minute and then tossed it toward the water. It fell short and landed on the sand, a good ten feet from the lake's edge. One of the dogs bounded toward it hopefully.

"Death is weird," she said.

"Yeah. I know." I stared hard at the lake. "I wish there was an alternative."

She gave a short laugh, the kind that means nothing is really funny. "Yeah, it's called living. Duh." She jumped off the picnic table, walked toward the lake and started throwing stones, trying to skip them along the water's surface.

I waited for a moment, watching her; then I followed her across the beach and stood at her side near the water's edge. Neither of us spoke for a long minute.

Karma dug in the sand with the toe of her sneaker. "What do you think happens? You know, after?"

I didn't think anything happened, but I wasn't sure I should say that. For all I knew, Karma thought her mother was watching her from heaven. Or believed that she'd turned into a star or been reincarnated as a fish. We'd never talked about it. "I guess there's really no way to know," I said at last.

"No. But I figure that when you die, everything probably just ends." She looked at me and wrinkled her nose. "It's strange. I guess it doesn't really make any difference what happens next. It wouldn't really change anything."

"Sure it would." I'd be less afraid, I thought, if I could believe in something.

"Not really. You'd still just have this one life here. You'd still be leaving everything you know."

I looked sideways at her. "So you don't think your mom is still out there somewhere?"

"Not really. No."

I watched her pick up another stone and a glimpse of something shiny caught my eye. I picked it up and brushed the sand and dirt from it.

"What's that?"

I held it out to her: a tiny, perfect silver cat.

"Huh." She looked at it for a moment and handed it back, losing interest. "Some kid must have dropped it." She crouched low and hurled her stone toward the water, and it skipped across the surface in a series of random bounces. "Five, six, seven!" She gave a loud whoop. "Yes! Got it! A new personal best, Dylan!"

I studied the little cat. It was curled up, its tail wrapped around its body. All it needed was a little cushion to lie on and it would be perfect for Casey's dollhouse.

❧

That night, I had just gotten into bed when Mom knocked on my door.

"What is it?"

"I wanted to talk to you." She sat down on the edge of my bed and studied my face. "About Casey."

"Oh." I dropped my eyes and wished the reading light on my bedside table wasn't so bright. There was a long silence. Obviously she was waiting for me to say something, but I didn't know what to say. Anyway, she was the one who said she wanted to talk.

"Obviously we're all hoping that Casey will be okay. But if she isn't okay...if this really is a relapse..." Her voice trailed off.

"You think I should see her, don't you?"

Mom didn't answer right away, and when she did, her voice sounded all thick, like she was swallowing the bigger half of what she wanted to say. "I just don't want you to have regrets."

"Mom?"

She didn't say anything, but her eyes were suddenly full of tears.

"You're not crying about Casey, are you? What is it? What's wrong?"

She shook her head. "Just some regrets of my own, I guess."

"About what?"

"Oh, Pickle. Stuff that happened a long, long time ago."

"Like what? What stuff?"

"I feel like I've caused this whole mess. Not telling Mark about you, not telling you more about him." She shook her head. "No point in dragging up the past." She wiped her fingertips across her eyes. "Sorry. I meant to talk to you about Casey."

"I don't want to talk about it."

"What's bothering you? That she's…that you guys are related? Or that she's sick?"

I shook my head. "It's just so weird that we're all going to die."

" 'To die would be an awfully big adventure,' " she said softly. "You know who said that?"

"No."

"Peter Pan."

I laughed; then I sighed. "But I don't want to die."

"No." She was quiet for a moment. "Hang on a sec, okay? I've got something I want to read to you, but I have to find it."

"Okay." I flopped back against my pillow. All of a sudden I felt incredibly tired.

Mom left and came back a couple of minutes later, holding a card in her hand. "It's a poem I wanted to read to you. It's short, don't worry."

"I'm not worried."

"Okay, here goes. It's part of a poem by Edna St. Vincent Millay. Do you know her?"

"No. Well, the name sounds sort of familiar."

She cleared her throat. "I feel kind of silly reading poems out loud."

"Just read it."

"Okay. Um, here goes. *Down, down, down into the darkness of the grave / Gently they go, the beautiful, the tender, the kind; / Quietly they go, the intelligent, the witty, the brave. / I know. But I do not approve. And I am not resigned.*"

I let the silence sit for a moment. A lump was swelling in my throat and I didn't trust my voice. "That's exactly how I feel," I said at last.

"I think it's how everyone feels."

"Where's the poem from? I mean, what's the card?"

Mom looked at me for a long moment. "It's from my mother's funeral. My dad read it. I've kept it…it was in a box in my closet."

The top two buttons on her white shirt were undone, and her chest was getting all red and blotchy, just like mine does when I get upset. "There's a lot of stuff that I don't like to remember," she said. "When you were little, it just seemed easiest to say that Mark was no one special. He wasn't going to be in our lives anyway."

"But it wasn't true."

"No. It wasn't. But later, when it started to matter to you, I felt like I was sort of stuck with my story. And the more time that went by, the more impossible it seemed to explain how it really was."

My mom had to be the only person in the world who would think that telling your kid she was conceived in a

one-night stand was preferable to the truth. "Was he…
was he your first boyfriend?" I held my breath, scared
that she'd suddenly stop talking, that she'd shut me out
like she always had before.

"My first serious boyfriend, yeah. He was a couple of
years older than me, and absolutely gorgeous. Dead sexy.
I was crazy in love. I quit school, ran away from home,
moved in with him." She gave a short laugh. "In this big
old house in the east end of Hamilton, with all these
people who came and went."

I studied her face and wondered if I'd know whether
she was telling me the truth or not. "You guys *lived*
together? For how long?"

"A year. A year of doing way too many drugs and
generally screwing up my life."

"But you were together for a whole year?" I hadn't
made it past the one-week mark with Jax.

"Yup. It wasn't a big accomplishment, baby. It was a
rotten year. I got a crappy job at a convenience store and
Mark did some construction work, but some of the time
we could barely afford to eat. My parents were furious.
I hardly spoke to them for months."

"And then your mom died." I couldn't imagine it.

"Yeah. And Mark broke up with me." Mom gave a short
laugh. "Just a month after Mom's accident. No real reason.

He just said he wanted to move on. He felt like I was holding him back."

I started to say something, but she shook her head and held up a hand, palm out, telling me to wait. "No, you know what he said? God, I can't believe I can still remember this. He said, 'I can't be with you and still have room to be who I want to be.'" She snorted. "Isn't that the most pretentious crap you've ever heard?"

I shrugged noncommittally. It actually kind of made sense to me, though dumping someone right after her mother died was pretty harsh. Still, what was freaking me out was the way Mom sounded like all this had just happened last month, not half a lifetime ago.

"It was bullshit. Having room to be who he wanted to be really just meant being free to have sex with Lisa Fleeting. Which I'm pretty sure he was already doing anyway. I kind of fell apart over it all. Sheri was living with us—Karma's mom, you know?"

I nodded.

"So we both moved out of the house and rented a room in an old dive of a hotel downtown. Sheri was dealing drugs. Not a good scene." Her eyes looked foggy and faraway. "We both got into some pretty messed-up stuff."

"And so...and then...?" I didn't know what I was asking. I just didn't want her to stop telling me the truth.

She gave a soft laugh. "And then I realized I was pregnant. It made me turn my life around, you know? Get my head straightened out, figure out what really mattered."

"Did you tell your dad?"

"Yeah. He wrote me a check and told me he never wanted to see me again."

"That's so *awful*." I couldn't imagine how someone could do that to his own kid. My mom might freak out if I got pregnant, but once she got over the shock, I knew she'd do whatever she could to help. Toni's mom would be like that too. Supportive.

She nodded. "Yeah. Well, he had a lot of problems."

"Still…"

Mom looked at me, her head tilted to one side, her gaze thoughtful. "I know, Pickle. But it's sort of funny, in a way. He thought my pregnancy was this terrible thing, but really, it probably saved my life. I quit doing drugs—well, the hard stuff anyway—and hitched a lift out west with some friends. Got an apartment, got a waitressing job, tried to make a life that I could imagine bringing a baby into. Being pregnant was the one good thing that came out of the whole mess. It was the one thing worth holding on to."

I could taste salty tears in the back of my throat. I wanted to tell my mom I loved her, but I couldn't quite say it. "I'll go and see her," I heard myself say instead.

My voice sounded tinny and strange, and I cleared my throat. "I'll go and see Casey."

◌

Mom called Mark on his cell phone first thing the next morning. Eight o'clock. "How is Casey doing?" I asked when she put the phone down.

"She's stopped throwing up and her fever is down. So she's feeling a lot better, but they won't know whether she's relapsing until they repeat the bloodwork. That poor kid must be getting so many needles, I can't imagine it."

"They still don't know?"

"I think they're just waiting to hear back from her last tests. Mark said that if her blood counts are still low by the end of this week, they might do a bone marrow biopsy to find out for sure."

I winced and tried to focus on the positive. "She's feeling better. That's got to be a good sign, right?"

"Let's hope so," Mom said. "That's all we can do."

"I guess." Maybe, maybe not. There were three more days until we should hear about my test results. Then maybe I'd be able to do more than just hope.

"Pickle? Do you want...? I can drive you there after school, but perhaps you should go in on your own."

I looked at her. "No, it's okay. You can come in with me."

She hesitated. "I don't want to intrude. You're family. I'm not. And Lisa might prefer it if I wasn't there, you know."

"Not really, no. I don't think they'd care. I'm sure they're expecting you to come too." So weird that Mom would be uncomfortable with Lisa after all this time. I wondered what Lisa had been like when they were all teenagers. She seemed so middle-aged compared to my mother. "Mom?"

"Yeah?"

"Has it always been…has Mark always had money? And you not had money?"

She looked startled. "That's a weird question."

I shrugged defensively. "I just wondered."

"No." She cleared her throat. "My parents were reasonably well off, actually. I assume Dad still is. Though he might have drunk his way through it by now. Asshole."

She was one to talk. It drove me crazy how there was always money for beer and wine, even when the phone bill was unpaid and we couldn't put gas in the car. "What about his family? Mark's, I mean?"

"Oh, they had money. He wouldn't take money from them though, not back in those days." She laughed, like something had just occurred to her. "He used to pocket extra packets of ketchup at fast-food places, mix them with hot water and call it soup. It was like he was proud of being so stubborn."

"Why was he? I mean, why wouldn't he take their money?"

"Pride, I guess. He didn't get along with his father." She shook her head. "I guess he must have got over it though, if his parents put him through law school."

"Did they?"

"Oh, I assume so. That's what they always wanted him to do. They were both lawyers."

"They're my grandparents, you know." It was a strange thought. I'd never met any of my grandparents.

Mom snorted. "I don't imagine they'd be too happy to hear it."

I curled my fingers inside my palms and clenched my fists tightly. If I saved Casey's life, they might be.

THIrTY

In the pediatric ward, Mom and I walked down the hallway, and I did my best not to be too obvious about my curiosity. A teenage boy, tall and skinny, walked by us holding on to an IV pole. By the nurses' station, a uniformed woman handed a crying baby back to a tired-looking mother. I peeked into a few rooms as we passed them, but blue sheets hung around the beds, hiding the occupants.

"Right here, I think," Mom said. "Room twenty-one." She hung back and let me go in ahead of her.

I slipped through the open door. Mark wasn't there, but Lisa was sitting in a chair and Casey was lying in the bed, propped up on a pile of pillows. She didn't have a hat on, and the combination of her baldness and the narrow, tight-sheeted hospital bed made her look both younger and sicker than when I saw her before. In the loose hospital pajamas, her bare arms stuck out like sticks, and I realized how skinny she was despite her round cheeks.

"Hey, Casey."

She held up a pink book. "Look what Mom brought me."

"Cool. Have you read it?" Or maybe four-year-olds couldn't read? I stepped closer so she could show me the pictures.

Casey flipped pages. "It's stickers. There's all the princesses in here."

"Oh…all the princesses?"

"Disney princesses, she means," Lisa said. "You know, Cinderella and Ariel the Mermaid and Beauty…" She trailed off, shrugging. "Anyway. Mark just went to get coffee for us both, but he'll be back. He wants to talk to you."

I nodded. I wasn't sure if I wanted to talk to him. I turned to look at Mom, who was still standing in the doorway, shifting from one foot to another. She and Lisa seemed to be ignoring each other, both waiting for Mark to come back before starting a conversation.

I sat on the edge of the bed and bent my head to look at Casey's book again. "So. Who's your favorite princess?"

∾

"Oh good. You made it." Mark walked in a few minutes later, a paper cup of coffee in each hand. "Sorry, Amanda. I guess I should have got three."

Mom brushed the words away. "How's everything going?"

I looked up at him and my breath caught in my throat.

Mark smiled. "So far today we've got good news, and more good news. Which do you want to hear first?"

I didn't think I'd really seen him smile before.

"Casey's still in remission," he said. "The doctors think she just had a virus."

Lisa nodded, looking at me. "Her neutrophils and platelets are coming back up."

Casey handed me a sticker of the Beast. "You can have this one if you want."

"Thanks."

She nodded matter-of-factly. "I don't like him. He's ugly."

I guessed she'd missed the message of that particular fairy tale. "Thanks. Um, Casey? I'm so glad you're feeling better." My voice wobbled a little. I really didn't want to start crying in front of everyone. I took the sticker from her and put it in my pocket. My fingers bumped up against something smooth and cool. The silver cat. "Here." I handed it to her. "I found this. Thought you might like it."

Casey's face lit up. "A kitty? For my house?"

"I thought maybe we could make a little cushion for her to sleep on."

She balanced it on her knees. "He can sleep with me. You want a princess sticker? You can have a Jasmine one. Not to keep though."

"So what's the second good news?" Mom asked.

Mark grinned again. "You want to tell them, Case? Tell them the news?"

She shook her head. Her tongue was sticking out slightly in concentration as she tried to peel a sticker from the book without dislodging the cat from his perch. "You tell them."

"We've got a bone marrow match," Mark said. "We're going back to Ontario and Casey's going to get her bone marrow transplant."

There was a sudden clutch in my chest and I gasped out loud. "That's so great." I put my hand on Casey's arm. "Casey, that's wonderful."

She didn't look all that interested.

"It is." Mark lowered his voice. "There's still a long road ahead, of course. But this gives her a chance, a good chance, of really beating this thing."

"Wow." I couldn't believe it. I found myself thinking of the poem Mom read to me: *I do not approve, I am not resigned.* I was actually going to be able to do something for Casey, not just stand by helplessly and watch her die. "So what happens now?"

"We'll fly back to Ontario as soon as we can arrange it, and as soon as she's well enough to travel."

Of course. They'd be leaving. "How soon can she have the transplant?"

"It'll take a few weeks, probably, to get everything set up. Once arrangements have been made to harvest the bone marrow from the donor, Casey will be admitted to hospital in Toronto for her treatment to prepare for the transplant. All in all, it shouldn't be more than a month or so."

Something wasn't making sense. I looked from him, to Casey, to Mom. "The donor? But…"

"Sorry, I wasn't clear. We got a match through the bone marrow donor registry. An anonymous donor. We'd almost given up on it ever happening."

"I thought…what about my tests?"

"We haven't got the results yet." Mark put his coffee down on a wheeled table beside Casey's bed. "We wanted to try every possibility, but the odds of you being a match were pretty remote."

"I'm really happy for you and for Casey. I mean, that's great. Really great." I stopped talking before everyone heard the wobble I could feel in my voice. They didn't need me anymore. I suddenly felt like we didn't belong here, like we were strangers intruding on this family we didn't even know. "I guess we better go," I said. I stepped closer to Casey. "Can I give you a hug goodbye?"

She nodded and held her arms up. "Bye, Dylan."

I put my arms around her. She felt smaller and more fragile than she looked.

"You don't have to rush off," Mark said. He was frowning, those two vertical lines deepening between his eyebrows.

I wondered if I'd ever hear from him again.

I looked at my mother. "Let's go."

"Dylan..." She picked up her purse and slung it over her shoulder. Then she hesitated, looking at Mark.

"Please, Mom."

She looked at me and nodded. "Okay."

We left without looking back, walking back down that long tiled hallway, past nurses and IV poles and dinner carts and visiting families. Mark hadn't tried to stop me leaving. He hadn't even said goodbye.

❦

Mom drove most of the way home without saying a word. I kept glancing over at her, but I couldn't tell what she was thinking.

I wasn't even sure what I was thinking. I leaned my head against the seat back. I should be happy. Casey had a shot at making it. And maybe I wasn't going to be the one to help her—or end up with a dad or a new set of grand-parents—but I wasn't losing anything either. I wasn't losing anything except a fantasy about my father.

Being angry with him was a relief in a way. It was less complicated than whatever else I'd been feeling.

I studied Mom's hands resting lightly on the steering wheel. The hummingbird's green wing tip poking out from beneath the black sleeve of her sweater. "Did you really get that tattoo when you were pregnant with me? Because of my heartbeat, like you said?"

Her cheeks flushed dark. "You saw Mark's tattoo."

I nodded. "Same as yours."

"Baby. Oh…" Her eyes were suddenly shiny. "I'm sorry."

"Why did you lie about it? You didn't have to do that."

"So stupid. I was so stupid." She shook her head. "You know, you were maybe three when you first asked me about that tattoo. And I told you all about humming-birds and how tiny they are, and how fast their hearts beat, and how their wings are just a blur when they hover in the air…" She stopped and smiled faintly.

"And?"

"And you were so sweet. You had your pajamas on, blue stripey boy's ones, and you had your swimsuit on overtop because it was new and you wanted to wear it."

"You remember what I was *wearing*?"

"And I picked you up and I could feel your skinny little ribs—you were such a scrawny kid, I always worried people would think I didn't feed you. Teenage mom, you know? People have such *attitudes*. Anyway, I picked you up and I could feel your heart beating. And I just made up that story. I think I wanted it to be true. It was a much better story than the real one."

I blew out a long exasperated breath. "Mom. You can't... you can't do that. You can't just pick what you want to be true." Although really, Mom did that all the time: *Scientists will figure out how to stop climate change. Sheri's in a better place now. I don't really drink that much.*

She turned to look at me wonderingly. "You know, I'd almost forgotten it *wasn't* true. I'd forgotten Mark had the same tattoo."

"Yeah, well. Maybe if you could stick to the truth from now on?"

She sighed. "So now what?"

"What do you mean?"

"Do you want to see him again? Or do you just want things to go back to normal?"

Back to normal. I figured that was probably what Mom wanted. Outside the window, the late afternoon sun hung low in the sky. I watched the telephone poles flicker past. One, two, three…I wasn't sure what I wanted. "It isn't really up to me, is it?"

"Isn't it?"

"I don't know if Mark will want to see me again. I mean, now that he doesn't need me, you know?"

"His loss if he doesn't." Mom pulled into the driveway and put the car in park. She didn't say anything for a minute, just sat there with her seat belt still on. "Dylan? He wanted to see you two years ago. When he first found out about you. I should've told you, but…"

No point now in telling her I already knew. "Yeah, you totally should've. So why didn't you?"

"I panicked. Told him to stay away, stay out of our lives." She looked at me, made a face and shrugged. "All those years I'd spent trying to avoid even thinking about him. You know, when I went to Ontario to get Karma, I was terrified I'd run into him. Just being in the same *province* freaked me out."

"Why, though? I don't get it."

"I think I was scared of how I'd feel if I saw him. It was all mixed up with my mom dying and Dad cutting me off, and all the stupid things Sheri and I did. Stuff I feel kind of ashamed of, now. I'd made such a complete break from my old life, you know? It was like, the longer I avoided it, the bigger it all got. When he called two years ago, I thought I'd have a heart attack." She shrugged again. "Now that he's here and I've seen him, it's like all that fear was a big balloon and it just got popped."

"When he called this time, you let me see him. How come?"

"Because I'd felt guilty for two years," she said. "Anyway, he said if I didn't agree to let him see you, he'd contact you directly."

I almost laughed. "In other words, you didn't have a choice."

She shrugged and didn't say anything for a while.

"I told him about the pictures," she said at last. "I mean, that you had tried to get in touch with him. And that I hadn't sent them."

"You did? What did he say?"

She gave a laugh that was almost a sob. "He said if I still had them all, he'd really like it if I could send them."

I blinked hard and tried to swallow the lump that had suddenly swelled in my throat. "What did you say?"

"I said that was just too damn bad." She looked at me defiantly. "He really is an asshole, Dylan. I don't want you getting hurt by him."

"Like you did."

She looked startled. "You think this is all about me?"

"Isn't it?"

"Baby…Oh, I don't know anymore. The way he just showed up like this. Not that I blame him for wanting to do whatever he could for Casey, but…"

"You still think he's an asshole, don't you? Even though he wasn't much older than me when you knew him."

"I'm sorry if that isn't what you want to hear, but yeah. I really do."

"People change," I said. "People grow up. Anyway, he seemed like he was nice to Casey."

Mom frowned. "You think I'm being too hard on him?" She dropped her eyes, twisted her hands together and studied her fingers. "You think your life would have been better with him in it?"

"I think you should have given him a chance."

"There was a reason I didn't send him those photos, you know." She looked at me as if she knew what I was thinking. "Not because *I* didn't want to see him, Dylan. Because I love you. Because I honestly thought you'd be better off without him in your life."

"Do you still have all those photos? Did you keep them?" She nodded.

"Can I have them?"

"For Mark? Are you going to give them to him?"

I met her eyes. "Maybe. I haven't decided. But I think it should be my choice, not yours."

She cleared her throat. "They're in a box in my closet. I'll find them for you."

"Mom?"

"Yeah?"

"Turn off the engine, would you? You shouldn't leave it running in the driveway like that."

She turned it off, reached across and gave me a hug. "Dylan?"

I leaned into her, resting my head on her shoulder. "Mmm."

"We're okay? You and me?"

"Yeah," I told her. "We'll be okay."

⁓

That evening, up in my room, I looked at the business card Mark had given me. His email address was on it: mlwheatcroft@thomsondavylaw.com. I wondered what the *L* in his name stood for. Liam? Lorne? Larry? I wrote him about a dozen emails and deleted them all. Too sappy, too formal, too desperate, too offhand, too serious, too jokey... The one I finally ended up with was short, just a few lines.

Dear Mark,

I hope Casey is still doing well and that the transplant goes smoothly. Please tell her that I send hugs and hope to see her again soon. Maybe after she recovers you can visit us again. It'd be good to stay in touch.

Best wishes,

Dylan

I wondered if it was too unfriendly. I thought about signing it *Love, Dylan,* but then I decided not to. It didn't seem honest. The truth was, I loved Mom and Karma and Toni, but I barely even knew Mark. All we had in common was some DNA.

Then again, he had asked Mom for the photographs.

I searched his name online and found a bunch of law-related stuff. Committees he'd sat on, an article he wrote in some journal. One photograph, a formal head shot, on his law firm's website. I really did have his eyes and his chin.

My phone rang and I answered, expecting it to be Toni.

"Dylan? It's Mark."

"Oh. Hi." My heart was suddenly racing.

"You left so quickly, I didn't have time to say...well, anything."

"Sorry." I sat on the edge of my bed. "It seemed like it should be just your family there."

"Dylan." He hesitated. "I'd hoped that you might start to consider us family. But, well, I don't want to be pushy. Or, ah...to give the impression that I feel entitled to anything."

"Family? You and Casey?"

"All of us, really. Lisa would like to get to know you too."

"Mom thinks Lisa hates her."

"Why on earth would she? Lisa knows I lived with your mom before she and I met."

"She didn't know about me though," I pointed out.

"She's had a couple of years to get used to that. Actually, we'd talked about it and decided to get in touch again when you were eighteen. To contact you directly if Amanda didn't want to be a part of it. But then, with Casey getting sick..." He cleared his throat. "It wasn't the best way for us to meet. I'm sorry about that."

"Oh." I rubbed my ankle where my too-tight sock had left indented lines. "You would have got in touch anyway?"

"Definitely."

There was a long pause. "Mom told you I wanted to send you pictures, right?"

"Yes. She told me."

"If you still want them..."

"I do."

"Okay. Well, I'll just mail them, I guess?"

Mark answered my unspoken question. "We're flying out tomorrow evening. But if you have time, I thought maybe...Lisa will be here with Casey so I could..." He sounded as nervous as I felt. "Can I pick you up at school? Take you out for coffee? Or tea? You drink tea, right? Or maybe lunch?"

I held my breath for a few seconds, then let it out in a long steady exhalation. "Yes," I said. "Yes. You can."

❦

Mom was out on the porch, scraping the peeling paint off the wooden bench.

"You know, I was thinking I might paint the porch. These railings...green, do you think? Or purple?"

I ran my hand along the peeling wood railing. "You've been saying that forever."

She laughed. "I know, I know. I think I might though. And wind chimes, don't you think? There's a hook there already."

I glanced up at the overhanging roof. "It'd be beautiful, Mom. You should do it."

"Well, I think I will." She put her arm around me. "Oh, Dylan. Just look at that sky."

I looked out into the night. The lights of the city faded the stars, but they were still visible, a scattering of faint pinpoints of light. A full moon hung low and orange in the sky. "Yeah. It's beautiful," I said. I let myself lean against her, just a little bit. "I could help you with the porch. If you wanted, I mean."

"I'd like that." Her voice wobbled slightly.

"Mom? I just talked to Mark."

"You did?"

"I'm having lunch with him tomorrow."

"He called you?" She stepped away from me.

I looked up at her and nodded. "Did you know he was planning to get in touch with me anyway? When I was eighteen?"

She shook her head. "No. Did he tell you that?"

"Yeah." I was quiet for a minute, half expecting her to say something skeptical, but she didn't say anything. "I want to get to know him."

"I know you do."

"Is it okay? I mean, are you okay?"

"I'll be fine." She blinked and smiled at me. "I found the photos for you. The ones I didn't send. They're in the living room. In the shoebox on the coffee table." She cleared her throat. "If you want, you could give them to him tomorrow. Save you the postage."

❧

I took the pictures into my bedroom and spread them out on my bed, from oldest to most recent. The first five were school photos. There I was at eight years old, with a nervous smile and shoulder-length hair tied into two limp braids. Age nine, ten, eleven, twelve—getting older, taller, thinner; my hair longer each year, growing out the bangs; the plastic barrettes being replaced by plastic headbands; posed stiffly against that same blue background every year.

Age thirteen, the first family photograph, with me squeezed between Karma and Mom on the couch. I remember taking that one. It was only a month or so after Karma came to live with us, when I wasn't yet sure if she was family or not. And the last two pictures, at fourteen and fifteen, with Karma and me laughing as the camera's timer went off. I hadn't noticed before, but Mom's face in those last photos was sort of sad, her eyes shadowed, her smile forced. I wondered if she'd felt guilty, knowing she wouldn't send the pictures. I wondered if she'd regretted letting herself get trapped in her own lies.

I hadn't got this year's picture printed yet. I picked up my camera from my bedside table, turned it on and studied the photograph. Even on the small screen, I could see Mom's stiff smile, Karma's bored expression and my tense grin. I pushed delete. I'd give Mark the others, but I wasn't going to print this one. I'd bring my camera tomorrow, when Mark took me out for lunch.

If I wasn't too shy to suggest it, he could take this year's picture himself.

ACKNOWLEDGMENTS

Many thanks to the Canada Council for the Arts for their generous financial support during the writing of this novel. Thanks also to my hardworking and talented editor, Sarah Harvey, and to all the friends and family who read countless drafts, shared their thoughts and encouraged me to keep writing, especially Maggie Bird, Michelle Mulder, Cheryl May, Holly Phillips, Pat Schmatz, and Ilse and Giles Stevenson. I am so very lucky to have you all in my life.

ROBIN STEVENSON is the author of many books for teens and children. Her young adult novels, which include *Escape Velocity, Inferno, A Thousand Shades of Blue* and *Out of Order,* have been nominated for numerous awards, including the Governor General's Literary Award and the Sheila A. Egoff Children's Literature Prize. Robin was born in England and now lives on the west coast of Canada with her partner and son. For more information about Robin and her books, please visit robinstevenson.com.